Being a
BOSS
Like Ari Ross

Being a

Boss

Like Ari Ross

C.B. Russell

Published in the United States of America, 2018

ISBN: 978-0-9774231-8-7

Liberated Expression Publishing

www.liberatedexpression.com

This book is dedicated to
the little Black Girls all around the world
who are learning to LOVE themselves.

-Temecka and Cyleigh

Preface

Ari is a young Black girl with wild and naturally curly hair. She is suddenly uprooted from her beloved hometown of Chicago and moved across the country to hot and sunny Arizona—shortly after her tenth birthday. As she tried to embrace her new life, Ari began encountering challenges she that never imagined she would have to deal with back home—in Chicago. She learned how to adjust to a new way of life, make new friends, and attend a new school far away from her friends and family, whom she loved dearly. No day was ever the same, and Ari soon learned the move to Arizona would provide her with lessons in self-esteem, pride, tolerance, and self-acceptance as a young Black girl in an extremely different environment. Now, sixteen years old, Ari takes advantage of an opportunity to once again be forced outside of her comfort zone. Only this time, she does it for the good of those who are where she used to be.

This novel will inspire and uplift young, Black girls all around the world who find they have to deal with accepting their uniqueness while adapting to a new way of life. It will speak to girls who feel they are alone in some of the growth and development issues they must face from themselves, peers, and those around them. While going on Ari's reflective journey through life from Chicago to Arizona, young readers are also able to pick up new terminology. The novel provides a twist on language with the breakdown of phonetics for the reader to maintain comprehension every step of the way.

Will Ari ever consider Arizona as home? Will Chicago *always* be her only home? Will she learn to accept her *natural* curly hair? Will she always desire long straight hair like—her bestie—Sofie?

Chapter 1

Mom said, when I was born—as she flat-ironed my hair for the homecoming dance—I had a head full of curly, shiny, black hair. I was born at 10 o'clock in the morning, right after my *favorite* Aunt Shonnie and her boyfriend, Michael, left my Mom's side at the hospital.

"After you came on out into the world, the midwife just put you right up here," Mom said.

She tapped her chest—above her heart. I shifted in the lawn chair and rolled my eyes.

"...like I *really* care to hear this story, yet *again!*" I thought.

Every time she's feeling all nostalgic (no-stal-gic), she would tell me the same story. Uhhh, I was so over it but secretly loved to hear it from time to time. It showed a loving side of Mom that was kinda...mmm...well, ok. Especially, since I was officially a high school junior with a driver's license. Gosh, I could hardly believe it! I was really growing up and accomplishing things in life. Before you knew it, I would be *on my way* to *college*! Never would I have imagined—after all the initial drama—things would be so wonderful for me.

When it all began, things were up and down like a roller coaster! The last five years—to be more specific—were full of non-stop *drama*! Mom turned my life upside down when I turned ten. TEN! I am still adjusting to being uprooted (up-roo-ted) from my *entire* family to this day. My entire existence (eh-xi-tence) and identity had been tied solely to who I was at home in Chicago, IL.

I was so excited about turning the big girl age of five. Five was the magical number for me. I would finally be able to go to big kid school—a.k.a. Kindergarten—and not that baby daycare school. I was so overjoyed.

As soon as I made it to Bisbees Bumbling Bee Daycare, I told Ms. No, "Now that I am five, my Mom said I will be going to kindergarten."

Ms. No looked at me with that very excited and warm smile of hers.

"Well, Ms. Ari, we must get you ready to do your best with the rest of your soon-to-be classmates," she said.

My plan to escape the babies and join the big kids only lasted until Mom came for parent-teacher conferences. I remember that story because—like my birth re-enactment (re-in-act-mint)—Mom loved to tell *that* story time and time again. I honestly liked hearing the story because it made me think about how much of a coning (kon-ing), silly goose I could be. I'm digressing (die-gress-ing), sorry. So I don't leave you wondering, let's get back to this part of the story. At the parent-teacher conference (kon-fer-in-s), Ms. No spilled the beans. It went something like this, LOL:

"We are working really hard to get Ari on or above grade-level before she leaves us," Ms. No said. She flashed that excited, warm smile of hers at me.

Mom's face went super blank. She looked over at me and shook her head.

"I'm sorry...where is she going?" Mom inquired. She looked bewildered (b-will-derd). Ms. No was sitting across from Mom and me with Ms. Tasha—the director.

"Ari told us, now that she's five, she will be going to regular school for Kindergarten," Ms No said.

There was a moment of silence and then a great eruption (e-rupt-shun). The eruption was Mom. She erupted with a loud sound of laughter. Mom laughed so hard and not to mention loud. She was crying *real* tears.

Ms. No and Ms. Tasha were so confused. I could tell by the way they were looking back at us from across the table.

"I'm sorry. I am truly sorry. Ahem (uh-him), this lil con artist of mine ain't going anywhere," Mom said. "She convinced the two of you she was leaving?" She went back to laughing with tears spewing (sp-eww-ing) down her cheeks.

You see why I love hearing this one? *Ooober funny*, right? Of course, on the ride home, we had a moment of clarity and corrective behavior regarding fibbing, truth, expectations, and the reality of the situation. Simply turning five didn't entirely mean I'd be moving on to Kindergarten.

My mom is a single Mom. She explained that she needed to figure out how to make the move with such a tight and demanding work schedule. However, she reassured me—as she relived the tale—that I would make the transition (trans-sit-shun) once she figured everything out. Then we busted out laughing and crying all over again.

Sorry, I digressed (die-gress-d), but it makes me chuckle and reminisce (rim-i-nis) when I think about memories such as those. The ones I left back home in Chicago—*when mom uprooted my life!*

Chapter 2

Shortly after my tenth birthday party, the final agreed upon bash, Mom told me there was a chance that we would move to Las Vegas or Arizona. I say this was the "final" birthday bash because my parties were—what Mom called—productions. They could also be a bit expensive. But, hey, I'm a single kid. Now that things were about to change, we needed to start slowing down on the extravagant (ex-strav-a-gant) spending.

You are about to turn some momentous numbers in your teen years and you don't want to do everything before it's time.

I agreed, as long as "my day" continued to remain all about *me*!

"Ari, are you listening to me?" Mom asked.

"Next week, while you are on holiday break, we are going to check everything out before it's finalized," she said.

As we rode to Naanah's job (Naanah is my Grandma), she gave me some magazines about Arizona and Nevada to look through.

I overheard Mom and Naanah.

"Naanah guess what? We are going to Arizona!" I blurted out.

"For what?" Naanah inquired.

"We're moving," Mom said.

Naanah flashed a surprising look of concern and disbelief. She asked Mom about my unscheduled interruption/announcement.

"...just something I am considering, but nothing is final," Mom stated.

Holiday break came; we were packed and ready to head to the airport. I think I am really weird. Even as a ten-year-old, I loved to travel. I loved rolling my luggage through the airport in the midst of all the hustle and bustle of people traveling. I loved when Mom and I got to board early because I was still considered (kon-sid-erd) a small child. I even loved boarding the plane, being greeted by the flight attendant, and seeing the captain and co-captain sitting in the front of the big plane. I loved—and still do—sitting by the window and being asked by the flight attendant, *what would you like to drink?* It makes me feel like a celebrity. On one of our family vacations to Disney, we flew *first class!* Talk about celebrity treatment! I was in *Heaven!* Watch out, Hannah Montana and Cheetah Girls, here comes ARI!! I can be so silly sometimes.

I remember leaving for the airport on a brisk November day. My hair was flat-ironed perfectly. As I walked from the house to the garage—to load up my bag—it blew in the brisk autumn wind. My hair was really long when straightened. It flowed past my shoulders and down my back. I am often questioned if my hair is real or weave extensions.

Previously, my Great Aunt Jean asked me, "Ari, what kinda' hair did your mom use on you?"

At first I just looked at her. I was really confused by her question. It then dawned on me; she thought Mom added some hair extensions to mine. I laughed and told Aunt Jean that it was all mine. She flashed a look of surprise and then flooded me with compliments about how good it looked.

"Leave me a bundle of yo hair on the table," she joked.

We both laughed so hard that we cried. That sort of reaction made me love wearing my hair straight—even more. Don't get me wrong, wearing it naturally curly also works. That is, until it starts to make me look like the bride of Frankenstein, LOL.

As part of my airport ensemble (an-sam-bul), my scarf was wrapped exactly how my favorite Aunt—Aunt Shonnie—taught me; it protected my throat. My scarf matched my pea coat. Mom purchased me a new pea coat from my favorite store, *Gap,* for the trip. I also had a brand new Hello Kitty luggage roller bag; it was packed with everything I picked out from all my favorite stores. Since it was fall in Chicago and summer-like weather in Arizona, Mom said we needed a few things to get the real feel of our visit. I imagined, as I walked through the airport, being caught by paparazzi—mistaken for a young Disney star. Yup, *I wanna be famous. I wanna be a star. I wanna be in movies. When I Grow Up by* The *Pussycat Dolls* is one of my favs. I was "jet-set bound."

There I go, being silly and going off topic. That's my bad, LOL. Where was I? Oh, yes...our visit to Arizona. It definitely was not a trip meant for a ten-year-old. I wanted to check out all of their amusement parks, roller rinks, bowling alleys, movie theatres, pools, and cool places to eat—places that served sushi or even mussels. We did see *malls*. I couldn't wait to see if we had the same stores as back home. Instead, we stayed in a basic hotel, drove around for hours on end, looked at house after house, and *never* went near a freaking pool. Who arranged this *boring* trip?! How am I supposed to be excited about moving here when we have done *nothing—for me*? And *where* are all the *black* people at in this city; all I see are *white* people.

Is this really finna...yes...F-I-N-N-A, be my life?! Ughhhhhhhhhhhh.

Then finally, FINALLY, I caught a break. We went to the mall!! I could have passed out for anticipation—like Junie B Jones on a Sunday. There were so many people...people of all different kinds. I thought to myself, so *this* is where everybody hangs out—*the mall*. I was in such amazement; I stopped dead in my tracks to take in the view. I remember this because...well...my thoughts were—once again—interrupted by my Mom. She was telling me to keep up. I was so excited, relieved, and—most of all—I was *happy*! Well, that happiness did not last too long. After walking the entire mall, all we bought were *souvenirs*! I just gave up!

As an only child to my Mom, to avoid being spoiled and acting bratty, we have an arrangement. We agreed—and it still works to this day—as long as my behavior is appropriate, respectable, consistent, and grades are passing with A's and B's, she will consider my request for materialistic things. Leading up to the trip, I kept a pretty good track record, which is why the anticipation of doing what I desired to do was killing me. Even though I am an only child—with a good behavioral track record—I am not spoiled with *everything* I think I should have. My Mom definitely has the word "no" loaded at the top of her response-to-my-requests list. I don't really act like an only child. I spend a lot of time with Aunt Shonnie's four kids—my cousins. There are three boys and one girl, Jaya, who is a year younger than me.

For the first time in a long time traveling, it was just me. Usually, when Mom takes me on vacation, we invite another kid to come along with us. Being by myself, I kinda expected Mom to have an agenda prepared—just for me. ANNNNNT! Wrong! This trip was definitely not Ari designated, nor focused. And to top it all off, Mom said no pool; she was not in the mood to deal with my hair. BUMERRRRRR!

After our visit, which I secretly *loved*, we returned home. Life returned back to normal. I mean...who wears flip-flops *that* late in fall? I continued with school at Mary's Christian School. Mom continued to work and attend classes—at night and on the weekend—to earn her Master's degree. On the weekends, we would also continue to do our usual stuff—birthday parties, family gatherings, hanging out with friends, shopping, cleaning, relaxing, church on Sundays, movies, and more relaxing. We lived as if we were just going to stay put and be happy. Unfortunately, that did not happen at all.

Out Christmas shopping on a brutally cold and crisp, sunny day, we decided to sit down and enjoy some sushi. This is when Mom delivered the dreadful news.

"Soooooo, Ari...everything is finally in place. We will be heading out the beginning of January," she said.

I think my entire body froze like a snowman without his scarf.

"That explains everything," I thought.

Each day I would come home from school and slowly began to notice how things disappeared from their normal spots. Mom had been quietly preparing for this day like a squirrel preparing for winter. This would explain why it appeared that there were boxes popping up *everywhere* throughout the house! I felt like a soccer ball had just kicked the wind out of my chest.

Once she said those words, "it's final," we started spending more time than usual with friends and family over the course of the next few weeks. January arrived with bitter sweetness. We–Mom, Cousin Charles, and I—packed up the remainder of our three-bedroom home, loaded up a moving truck in the middle of the night, and hit the highway all in the blink of an eye. You know how movies rewind a scene in fast pace? Well, in my mind, it looked like that—until we were on the highway. In what I proclaimed as my corner of the moving truck, I made sure my belongings were neat, together, and secure. I even asked Mom if I could ride on the couch in the back of the truck to make sure my things arrived safely and in one piece. She just laughed and said, "Ari, *no*, I am not trying to catch a child endangerment case. I'm trying to upgrade your life, silly "

Cousin Charles said we would have to drive across lots and lots of highways—just to get there. The never ending highway was C-R-A-Z-Y. About an hour into our ride, Mom realized she *left the directions* on how to get to our new home in Arizona. Who does that?! She has this massive plan to move and forgets the directions. *You have got to be kidding me*! I thought it was a sign that we should not be moving. Nahhhh, she called my Aunt Trudy, and the rest is history. This lady *always* has a backup plan. *Geez*! To make sure we made it safely to Arizona, Naanah enlisted one of Mom's older cousins who was also a truck driver, Cousin Charles. He said this was perfect timing because he had always been interested in visiting Arizona. He also joked with Mom that maybe the lack of directions was a sign that we should stay put. Mom didn't look as if she found it amusing. Needless to say, Charles and I did. We laughed about it and grabbed some breakfast from McDonald's. Then we got back on the highway.

Road trips were not anything new to me. When I was eight, our entire family took a road trip from Chicago to Atlanta, South Carolina, Ohio, and Virginia. We stayed in different hotels, visited different malls, and ate at so many different places. Everywhere we went, we had a blast. I loved every minute of that road trip. Mom bought me *all* new clothes, and I wore my hair naturally curly that entire summer. Mom said it would be easier to maintain, especially since I would be in and out of pools all summer long. As I drifted off to sleep, I thought to myself, *this should be just like that. We will be there in no time.*

Chapter 3

Our early morning departure left no room for me to get all emotional about leaving *my life* (eye-rolling) behind. As we made our first stop to gas up and grab a bite to eat, I looked around and began to feel all these emotions and not to mention my legs. I couldn't believe what my Mom had just done to me. All of my excitement was slowly fading. I will have to make new friends *all* over again. I will have to get used to a new school *all* over again. What if they are mean? What if they don't like me? I mean...not having to wear a uniform is great, but what kinda clothes do they wear? Is it going to be hot *all* the time? What kind of music do they listen to in Arizona? Do they like

Notorious B.I.G.? Are they Bratz fans? Do they even know what an American Girl is? Wait, what about *church*? Will I be able to be on the Tween Praise Dance team? Do they even have a church like ours? So many questions that I did not have before...*now*, NOW, I have TONS. I felt like my life was spiraling out of control since turning 10. We could have just done it when I was on my way to *college* or something! My Mom just does *the most!* I let out a long, hard sigh, dropped my shoulders, ordered me some food from the Waffle House Restaurant, used the bathroom, and slowly climbed back in the truck to ride down more highways. At one point, I had taken all the naps I could, ate all the snacks I could, and played more games of i-spy than I care to admit.

"Ughhh, are we almost there?" I asked. "How much further do we have to go?"

Mom and Charles both laughed at me.

"We have about ten more hours to go. I'm sorry, Ari, but this is gonna be a long drive," said Mom.

"If you need to go to the bathroom, just let me know and I will pull over, okay?" said Charles. He winked. I think he noticed my look of sadness and desperation.

"How bout this...let's see who can spot the most 'Murphy Jones' trucks between now and the next exit we have to take," Charles stated.

"If you win, then cheeseburger on me," Charles said. "If I win, you have to take over the wheel, deal?"

"Deal," I replied.

I wanted to see if he was actually going to let me drive! That would be a good story to call and tell everybody—once we got there.

With pride, I can say that Charles lost. No driving but I definitely enjoyed a double cheeseburger with an Oreo milkshake on him. We drove, drove, and drove for the next few hours. Someone would call Mom and me every few hours to see where we were and how the drive was coming along. It made me feel special to know that most of our entire family was missing me, and I had just left. I smiled and fell back into yet another nap.

Before we finally made it, I remember pulling over to allow both Mom and Charles a few hours to rest up before we completed the last leg of the drive to our new home. Because I don't remember much—past it being dark—I think it's safe to say that I continued my nap. As we *finally* crossed the border into Arizona, we began to talk excitedly about what we saw, what we wanted to do, and sang every song we listened to—once we found the Black radio stations. I was really glad my hair was up in its natural curly ponytail. Once we crossed the border into Arizona, the temperatures went from being cold like at home, to hot like the summer. It was the middle of January—winter. By wearing my curly ponytail hairstyle, I kept cool. It was easy for me to sleep.

This may not seem like much of a big deal or an important decision, but when my hair is straight, the maintenance (main-ten-ance) requires several time consuming steps. I have to make sure it is moisturized and my scalp is not sweaty. Additionally, it has to be tied up in a scarf and covered by a bonnet. That's a lot of steps. So, to be able to just let my natural hair be free means, I only have to keep it moisturized and pulled back into a ponytail. I can lay any way I want. I don't have to tie it down or wrap it up. As I laid my eyes on the peaks of Arizona's mountains, I was amazed. This was better than seeing my first ever shooting star when we drove through Texas. It was as if I could reach out and touch it with my own bare hand. The grass was so vibrantly green and stretching as far as the eye could see. Now that I really consider it, the drive wasn't that bad.

As my eyes tried to capture every inch of the scenery, we started up a new, more exciting game of i-spy.

This must be what it feels like to be on a trip with a Mom and a Dad—given that it's just Mom and I.

We *finally* arrived to our Arizona home, and I was—along with my bladder—relieved. My immediate excitement of arriving completely removed my sadness of leaving. I was excited about our new apartment. All I could think about was my new bedroom with my very own walk-in closet that had sliding mirror doors, our patio overlooking the mountains, and the apartment complex having two free pools and a movie theatre. Needless to say, I was *ecstatic*! I could not wait until I could invite all of my friends and family out for a visit. We would *take over* bar-be-cueing, playing music, playing in the pool, watching movies in the theatre, and *shopping*.

Mom grabbed our keys, and we all worked hastily to unload the truck of belongings into our new home. As the weekend came to a close, we dropped Charles off at the airport to return home to Chicago. Once he gave us that final wave and hug good-bye, something within me began to lose the excitement that dwelled within me twenty-four hours ago. Judging by the look on Mom's face, I think she also felt it. We took a deep breath, buckled up, and headed home. Once we were home, we took a few calls and began to unpack our stuff. To make us feel more at home, Mom played some music off the CDs made by Aunt Trudy. We sang, danced, unpacked, and laughed our way around our new home.

Lying in bed, I began to wonder what everybody was doing back at home. Mom interrupted my thoughts.

"Ari, what do you want to eat for dinner before it gets too late?" she asked.

"I don't care; I don't really have an appetite," I said.

We ended up at Hooters for hot wings—my favorite. She was trying to cheer me up. I felt a tear drop down my cheek while I looked at the menu.

"This is really happening," I considered. "I will have to go to bed in a strange place and wake up without seeing Naanah, Aunt El, Aunt Trudy, Aunt Shonnie, Cordi, Nate, Jaya, or Azzi."

Normally, I spent my weekends at Naanah's while Mom went to work. There wasn't anything really special going on. It was just family being family. Naanah's home is really awesome. The attic has a big television on the wall with big comfy seats to sit in. She created a game room for us. It had a Wii so all the kids could play together. There was a Ms. Pacman arcade game, a hockey table game, board games, card games, and we each had our own Nintendo DS. There was a small office area where Jaya and I played "office" and "school" when we were tired of playing with the boys. We would also watch movies, eat, bar-be-que in the back yard, crack jokes, play UNO, sing, or just hang out in the backyard. I am really going to miss that and them. While eating my hot wings, Mom tried to make light of my long face by telling me that Naanah and Aunt Winne would be coming to visit us soon. She also tried to remind me that we would go *home* for summer break in a few months. *Being missed mean getting gifts*. I just shrugged my shoulders. She paid the tab, ushered me home to get ready for my first day of school, and conditioned my curly natural locks. To not look so sad, I began to think about what I would wear for my first day of school.

On the way home, I decided not to wear my curly afro to school; I'd wear it straight. I wasn't sure how these kids were going to look at me—the new *black* girl. To add a big curly afro might be too much.

"Mom, can you do my hair for me tonight," I asked.

"Ari, are you serious, it is already late and the box is not even unpacked yet," she said.

"Can we do it tomorrow, once you get out of school?" she countered.

"I don't want everybody staring at me. It's bad enough I am the new *black* kid," I mentioned.

She let out a long sigh.

"No crying, whining, ouching, scooting down in your chair or complaining. And you *must* wash your hair *thoroughly* three times, take your shower, lay your clothes out, and floss!" she said.

"Deal," I said.

We made it home and as promised, I cleared out my to-do list—*minus* the ouching. Mom is heavy handed. When rushing to finish up my hair, it felt like she was beating my scalp with that blow dryer brush, LOL. I did not complain because I really wanted to fit in on my first day of school.

Once she was finished, she told me to look at it in the mirror before putting my scarf and bonnet on and going to bed. I looked in the full-length mirror on the closet. I ran my hands down my super straight—once curly—mane and smiled. *Yup, this will work; we can introduce those curls later.*

Chapter 4

I took a deep breath and walked through the double doors on that dreadful first day at my new Arizona school, Rancho Cougar Elementary School. As I looked around at everyone moving hastily about—thinking this is *totally* different than Mary's Christian School back home—I was snapped out of my thoughts by a lady in a blue suit.

"Hello, I'm Principal Martin," she said.

I instantly clutched my brand new American Girl backpack and stared like a deer in headlights at the lady before me. With a huge grin on her face, she stuck her hand out.

"Hu...Um... Hi, I'm Arian, nice to meet you," I said.

A bell rang and kids began to form lines all around the playground. Teachers came charging from—what seemed like—every which a way.

"Pleasure. Can I assist you with anything?" Principal Martin asked.

"No, I think I'm good," I mumbled.

My mouth was so dry. It felt like I had just eaten a handful of sand, LOL. Good thing mom insisted I take a mint and not scare anyone off with "hot mouth." LOL. In my mind, I was thinking, *can we speed this lil process up?* I did not want to be late when I was already the new *black* kid on the block.

Great, if you need anything, there's staff that can be found pretty much everywhere; they will get you to where you need to be. Have a wonderful first day of school.

Sure, I was the new kid on the block, but what could have possibly given it away? Was it the dumb look I had on my face? Perhaps the fact that a little black kid was standing in the middle of the walkway and looking at the playground instead of being on it. Mom really tried to get me to wear my hair natural. All of our stuff was still in the process of being unpacked, and as she puts it even to this day, she *loves* my hair natural. I am glad our little compromise (kom-pro-mize)—and a pouty look—was all it took for her to straighten it.

As I stood looking with—what I am sure was—a bewildered look on my face, I didn't really see too many black kids running around or towards the playground. Why was I looking so bewildered? Well, how would you look if you walked into a new school and everyone around you looked as if they were behaving like animals recently released from captivity? The fact that I was standing there like a human—instead of running around wild like the other kids—was one easy way to see that I was new.

I began my move toward the rest of the kids.

I thought to myself, "Is this *really* my future life? Is this how life will be from now on—full of *White people*?"

Ok, I see one person who looks like me. Ooh, there's another one. Maybe I am being a bit racist. During our visit, Mom and Naanah made sure to visit potential (po-ten-chal) schools for me to attend. We visited each school, classroom, and collected a lot of paperwork before leaving. Before Mom dropped me off in the carpool line, she made sure I had my information down pat. I let out a deep sigh and joined the end of a—

now moving—line to room 303, Ms. Riley's 3ʳᵈ grade class. Everyone filed into the classroom and put their belongings away on their hooks. I just stood at the door watching the madness unfold. I believe, thinking about it now, I was in shock. Back at Mary's Christian School (MCS), we had lockers which were in our hallways. Hooks and cubbies? ...are we KINDERS?! Ari, chill out, this is not Chicago. Mom and I talked about this when she made her *grand announcement*.

"I can't believe we are moving to Arizona, Ari," she said.

I looked at her with a blank stare on my face. She looked back at me with an excited look on her face. She even had the nerve to ask me, *what do you think?*

"I don't know what I think!" I thought to myself. I felt a shiver go down my spine. Part of the shiver was due to the fact that we were outside shoveling snow in *freezing* cold weather—on a *Saturday*. The other part was because, at the age of ten, how would any kid feel being forced to leave all of their besties, family, and favorite fun places behind?! I suddenly felt the wind blow against my face, that shiver down my spine again, and the cold weather of Chicago. It changed my angry thoughts about moving to Arizona; it is sunny all the time.

Chapter 5

Moving—at ten—was probably one of the hardest challenges of my life. I just knew I would live in Chicago, *forever!* I began to think of some of the positives. Well, that was before I embarrassed myself in front of all these new people. Ms. Riley touched my shoulder, interrupting my thoughts. Geez, what is it with people around here? Let me give you the positives, and then we can catch up with Ms. Riley. There will be no more uniforms, which both Mom and I hated but made stylish. We get to go outside and have *real* recess. MCS did not have recess unless it was close to the end of school. Our school was one building, one classroom, no lunchroom, and—did I mention—

one uniform. I think you get the picture. I get to finally have lunch in a real cafeteria and pass from class to class like a real big girl. Instead of a book box, we have a library I can check out books from. Instead of taking a bus to the YMCA, we have real physical education. And best of all, this school takes *field trips!* YESSSSS! Maybe this school won't be *that* bad. Okay back to Ms. Riley.

"Morning. You must be Ari," she said.

I smiled, or at least hoped it looked like I smiled.

"Yes," I replied. I squeezed my backpack strap. I instantly thought, OH DEAR GOD, this lady is getting ready to put me on blast in front of the entire class! NOOOO! She showed me to a desk which had my name on it. Then she told me to *just* have a seat; my buddy will show me what to do.

"Did your Mom send you with your supply list?" she asked.

"Supply list...umm, yeah. I have supply stuff in my bag," I said.

Another bell rang. The announcements came on...then the pledge of allegiance. By this time, everyone was standing behind their chairs but me. I was looking around and thinking *should I stand up?*

Mary's Christian School was *totally black*. We had prayer in the morning then announcements by Mrs. G. Finally, we said the National Black Anthem—*not any Pledge of Allegiance* (a-lee-jance). To avoid looking like an outsider, I slid out of my seat and stood by my chair on the side of my new shoes—the way Mom hated because it *ruined* them. The pledge ended, and everyone sat down in one quick, robotic motion. *Last to rise and last to fall*, back into my seat that is.

I was seated next to a tall, freckle-faced blonde girl named Sofie. Ms. Riley came over and introduced us. She told me that Sofie would be my go to buddy until I became comfortable with class routines. Sofie eagerly said hi to me and asked where I was from.

"Chicago, IL," I said.

"Where's that? I've never been there before. I've only been to California," she stated.

Where is Chicago? In the 3ʳᵈ grade, you don't know where Chicago, aka CHI-TOWN, aka THE WINDY CITY is! Ari, *remember* what Mom said. *Things will be different. The people will be different; you are different. Be nice.*

You see, on that loooong ride to Arizona, Mom tried to address all that she believed would be beneficial (ben-eh-fish-al) to helping me make a smooth transition.

We talked about how there may be less of "us" around—black people. I personally prefer to be identified as Mocha, lol. We talked about how school would be different. I had been at a predominantly (pre-domi-nant-lee) black school with black teachers for the first 9 years of my life. She explained racism and when someone is being racist. She "encouraged me" to have an open mind and be friendly because "*we ain't movin back.*" We talked about how wonderful it would be to *not* have to wear our winter stuff anymore. Additionally, we discussed being able to swim whenever we wanted, not hearing gunshots, seeing the sun all day, e'r day, and exploring all that Arizona has to offer. For someone of such a young age, I swear some of our conversations were pretty sophisticated (so-fis-ti-kate-ed). Being an only child, allows for a lot more attention but in a big kid/teenager type of way. In fact, when I was two or three, one of Aunt Winnie's friends gave me a nickname, *teenage toddler.*

"Chicago is in Illinois," I said. "It's a really cool place."

Finally! It is lunch time! Sofie and I—along with the rest of Ms. Riley's class—sat together and ate our lunch. After lunch, the lunch ladies lined us up and took us out for recess. Recess is where I met all of Sofie's friends. Some of them became part of my ride-or-die clique. Third grade went on as third grade does, uneventful and full of learning stuff. Until one day, *THE DREADFUL INCIDENT* occurred. By the way, Mom and I decided to introduce them to the natural me. They turned me into an exhibit—ooohing and awwwing. They asked to touch my hair and even asked if it was a *wig!* I was *so* embarrassed and insulted. Most of all, I was *mad at mom!* She convinced me this would be a great idea. At the end of the day, once I cleared my streaming tears, I vowed to *never* wear my hair curly *again!* Having to go through the experience of educating "others" on me, my hair, and my culture, at ten years old, really made me angry and frustrated. It got to the point where it felt as if the only choice left was to *get straight ghetto on them.*

Where I come from, school is *extremely* important. *It is the way to become successful in life.* My Mom, back in first grade, took me aside and made it very clear—*failing is not an option in this house.* From that moment forward, I have earned *nothing* less than a B grade and take *great pride* in my academic excellence. On this day, Ms. Riley—now Mrs. Bailey—put me in a situation that forced me show my classmates, who had gotten on my last nerve, who Ari, the angry Black girl from *Chicago,* was.

Mrs. Bailey changed our seating over the weekend and put us in groups to work on math word problems. She sat me with kids whom I did not really care to neither deal with nor sit by. In my group was Shannon, Natalie, Angel, Me, and Vickie. Shannon and Natalie also sat at the table with me. They were *never* quiet! Mrs. Bailey is always taking table points away from us because of *them.* Today was no different. Shannon and Natalie were just talking, laughing, and playing non-stop. We—Angel, Vickie, and I—tried several times to get them to at least stop talking. We even tried giving them the easy problems. They refused then made comments about how we were trying to tell them what to do. Our group received several warnings to stay focused. Shannon and Natalie just would not stop. They were really starting to push my buttons. Immediately after Mrs. Bailey gave us our groups, I asked her—in private—if I could go to another group when we did math circles. She refused to switch me.

As we began to work on our second set of math problems, I'd already become annoyed with my group mates. I sighed in sadness, dropped my head, and decided I was just going to sit in the group and do my work. The minute we got back into math groups, Shannon and Natalie instantly started goofing off again. *Can you guys just stop for a second and get some work done*, I thought. I was getting Chi-town angry. Chi-town angry is when you just explode and say *all* the mean things you have been holding back, regardless of how it hurts the other person. It's said in an extremely loud and animated way—fingers in your face, neck rolling, eye-rolling, and almost face-to-face screaming. A few drops of spit fly out every once in a while. Chi-town angry is when you let the other person—or people—know; the next step is a butt whoopin with *no regrets*. I went back to Mrs. Bailey to plead my case and avoid snapping on those silly white girls. Suggesting we work on communication and compromise, she refused to move me. When I got back to the group, they were still at it. Now...they were putting a note in our agendas for our parents to sign— acknowledging bad behavior. I was freaking out. This was Mrs. Bailey's threat. I threw a tantrum so bad, Azzi would have been proud.

"You guys are being so stupid right now," I said. "I wish I was never put in this stupid group; y'all get on my nerves and make me *sick*. All ya'll do is talk about *dumb boys* and *stupid* Disney Stuff! *Who cares? We are supposed to be* WOOOOORRRKING!!!"

By this time, the entire class was quiet and looking at me and my big black curly afro. They were probably looking at the group as well, but all I saw were eyes on me. Mrs. Bailey looked a little bit pale and probably was even afraid. She cleared her throat and sent me into the quad where the classes connected and teachers ate lunch to cool off. She also made me call my Mom, requesting a meeting after school to discuss my behavior. At lunch, I sat to myself, crying, eating, and angrily wiping away my tears. Sofie tried to console me, but I was not in the mood. I was missing everyone and everything about home. I questioned why we had to move to stupid Arizona. I questioned how being so far away from my family, school, friends, and comfort was good for me. At recess, I went to the farthest end of the field and cried my heart out. Every mean thing that happened each day in class, at lunch, and at recess was on my mind. People were making fun of how I speak, look, eat, and what I know and don't know. Even when I wore my hair in a curly afro, they were always asking to touch it. The boys were especially mean. I hated it. They said I looked like the fat Oprah Winfrey—just *mean*!

Mom came rushing into the classroom. I sat at the horseshoe table. I was with Mrs. Bailey. As she greeted both Mrs. Bailey and me, she sat her bag down and looked at my face—red with tears streaming down my cheek. She sighed and leaned back into the small chair that caused her knees to hit the table.

"Hey, Ari, what's wrong?" Mom asked.

She asked in a concerned, *you betta not have gotten in trouble* way. Mrs. Bailey explained what happened during math. Mom had a confused look while Mrs. Bailey was talking.

"I'm sorry, who threw a tantrum," she asked.

"Ari," Mrs. Bailey replied.

"Wait, I'm sorry. This Ari right here?" she inquired.

"Yes," Mrs. Bailey said.

Mom then turned to me.

"Ari what's going on?" she asked me.

I began to tell my Mom about the table troubles and what happened in our Math group.

"Where did that come from?" Mom asked.

"I wasn't going to get in trouble for them not doing their work," I replied. "I told them in the lunch line—when they were making fun of how serious I am about doing work—I am from Chicago and *this* is how I am."

Mom looked as if she was gonna start crying. I told her how some of the boys were making fun of my hair when I wore it naturally—the reason I kept asking her to flat iron it. I finally said what I was feeling. *I wish we had just stayed at home. I hate it here.*

Mom instantly apologized to Mrs. Bailey. She turned directly to me.

"First of all, we are not moving back," she said. "I am sorry you are having a hard time adjusting, and it will get better. I promise."

She said I cannot be in the classroom scaring those little white people. *Telling them you from Chicago and that is how you are...that is not who you are or how you are!* She said Mrs. Bailey probably didn't have a clue of what to do with me at that point. *Tantrums are not what we do. We use our words to communicate our feelings. If we feel that we are not being heard with respect, we wait for the proper time and have the proper conversation.* She then talked with Mrs. Bailey about not changing the groups. While this tantrum was extremely rare for me, it was all that I felt I could do to avoid punching those girls in the face. On Monday, we all had new seats.

Once we were alone, Mom and I talked about how people—in general—can be mean. Mom explained that sometimes...I can be a bit intimidating to others...others who don't know just how smart and talented I am because of the frown on my face. Mom then looked me square-dead in my face and said *no matter what people of any race say about your hair, you are BEAUTIFUL. Your hair is beautiful and they wish they had your hair.* She also promised to flat iron my hair once a week. The one condition was that I wore my hair natural at least twice a month. We agreed we needed to find the right stuff to make my curly locks look less like an afro. I was not going to *stop* wearing my natural hair that we both love. She also made me promise, *no more tantrums.* If I am put in that type of situation again, I'll do my part and grab me a book to read quietly.

It was a sweltering 105 degrees. We decided to have dessert—frozen yogurt—before dinner. In that moment, I still felt moving here was a huge mistake.

"Guess what?" Mom asked.

"We are moving back home," I said.

She dropped her wrist with her spoon and looked at me with a smirk.

"*No,*" she replied. "Naanah and Aunt Winnie will be here this weekend."

"*Yess,*" I said.

I missed my Naanah so much! Aunt Winnie was cool too. We headed to the store and then home to do our normal evening routine. We marked the calendar to Naanah and Aunt Winnie's visit. I reminded Mom she promised to straighten my hair. Tomorrow, them dumb boys gone be looking stupid. *Curls gone and hair flowing down my back*, I thought to myself. For the first time in weeks, sleep felt so good.

Chapter 6

I was so excited to see my Grandma and Aunt. We were off to pick them—and two of Naanah's golfing friends—up from the airport. Thankfully, they were there on a weekend, when I had an extra day off. We dropped everyone off at the hotel. The flight landed so late. Mom let me spend the night with Naanah and Aunt Winnie in their hotel room. She promised to meet us in the morning for breakfast. I tried to stay up while Naanah and Aunt Winnie unpacked their belongings and changed for bed, but the waiting and anticipation of their visit—plus the chain of events at school—had really wore me out. One minute I was talking to Naanah about school, the next I was waking up to Mom and Aunt Winnie's voice. Naanah left early to go golfing with her friends. Mom had two outfits laid out for me to choose from once I came out of the bathroom. She and Aunt Winnie were catching up on everything that happened since we moved.

Once dressed, we headed out the door to explore Arizona. I enjoyed Aunt Winnie. She was fun and loved to shop and eat like Naanah. Aunt Winnie, like my Mom, was all about school—so was her conversation. Mom just had to tell my business about the "tantrum." Aunt Winnie didn't lecture me. Instead, she told me not to let them lil white kids intimidate me. She looked me directly in my eyes.

"Just focus on showing them *just* how much smarter you are than them. God will take care of their wrong doings, Ari," she said.

"Yes, Ma'am," I replied.

"Speaking of the Lord, have you all gone to church since being here?" she asked.

I just looked at Mom on that one and focused on my Oreo milkshake.

Once Naanah and her friends were done golfing, they met us at the restaurant. Then we headed to show them our new apartment, the gated complex, and all the fun things I liked about it. We grabbed a few overnight items and headed back to their hotel. Back at the hotel, we chilled by the pool and ordered room service. Tomorrow, we would spend the entire day together— shopping. Naanah let me get whatever I asked for. That went against my Mom's wishes. As we shopped, with and without Mom and the rest of the group, we talked about how I felt like the spotlight was always on me— the lil black, curly afro girl. Naanah told me that people are fascinated by the unknown. Let them get to know you a little bit and they will begin to see you for you. She and Aunt Winnie said they can even be ignorantly curious because of what they learn from movies and television shows about black people being loud, explosive, stupid, showy, and criminals. They encouraged me to show them what Chi-town is all about—through my eyes and in a good way.

I loved my conversations with Aunt Winnie and Naanah because they weren't unsophisticated. They talked to me in a teenage manner. I liked that a lot. It made me feel as if my words were important. After shopping, we all took a break, changed our clothes, and headed out to a fancy dinner. Mom re-flat ironed my hair; it had started to curl from the heat. We ate sushi as an appetizer. Then I had chicken as a meal and an ice cream sundae for dessert. After such a long day, I was pooped. I didn't even put up a fight when Mom told me that my bags and I would have to come home with her. There's nothing like shopping to cure the aches of being homesick.

The next day, Sunday, Mom was up banging and clanging pots around.

"Good Morning, Ari," Mom said. "Since I am cooking Sunday dinner for everyone, it's cereal for breakfast."

"Ok," I replied.

In my room, as I ate my big ol' bowl of cereal, I dumped all of my new stuff onto the bed. As I began to look at each piece, I heard Mom yelling how I needed to put my stuff away and clean my room and bathroom by two.

"O-K!" I said—in between spoonfuls.

For Sunday dinner, Mom made fried chicken, tilapia, baked mac n cheese, sweet potatoes, greens, cornbread, black-eyed peas and a chocolate cake. It was all made from scratch. Cooking is one thing my Mom is the best at, and that is the truth, Ruth. We said prayers over the meal and dug in several times. Once we were done eating, the *Itis* (eye-tis) set in. We were laid out all over the place. I felt just like I was back at home. This is what we did *every Sunday*. I, on the other hand, was scared to give in to the food coma. I didn't want to wake up to find Naanah and Aunt Winne gone. To no agreement, the food coma won me over.

After everyone was done napping, we had more dessert and headed out for a drive back to the hotel. Naanah and Aunt Winnie began to pack, do their flight check-ins, and review all the deals they found at the malls we visited. "Well, Ari, you only have two more months before you'll be home for summer break," Naanah turned and said. "Hopefully, when you get back to school, things will be a lot easier for you."

I could only agree, but things looked as if they were *not* going to get any better. Naanah made me promise to send her a funny card each week until we returned home for the summer. She said that once she gets mine, she will send me one back. They may even contain a little surprise in them. This excited me all the more. Mail and money...YES!

Instead of dropping everyone off at the curb, like we did when we dropped Charles off, we went inside. Mom parked, helped unload the luggage, and we all walked inside like we were all leaving. I smiled as I walked. I carried Naanah's carry-on bag for her and pretended the big bag was my purse to those walking by. Remember, I love traveling and being in the airport. When I took a peek at Mom's face, she even looked a bit sad. I thought to myself, *finally*. She had been so happy and positive; she finally showed that she *was* sad. Once we got to the security checkpoint, we gave everybody a hug good-bye. Naanah slipped a twenty in my pocket as she gave me a hug; see, she's the bestest. Aunt Winnie put five dollars in my hand after she gave me a hug. Mom and I stood waving as we watched them. After we could not see them anymore, Mom checked the flight board, watched a few planes take off, and sighed.

"Come on, let's go," she said.

I think I even saw her wipe a few tears away. For me, it was no secret; I was sad. When she looked at me, I was crying. She tried to console me with a hug. She suggested that we indulge in two of our favorite past times—the mall and eating. We went to Build-a-Friend and a new place to eat from our list of places to try. We both knew and remembered all those leftovers back at the house but were in no mood to be reminded of the time we just had with our family. Mom always knows how to heal a wound.

One Saturday, while we were at the mall, my Mom decided to stop in this really expensive-looking hair and body product boutique. This was in search of something to give my hair *all-day shine* and not *afternoon knaps*, LOL. Mom talked to the sales lady and we walked around the store reading the different bottles of products. Unlike back home, the sales lady asked if we would like to try a sample of any products—before we bought them. Mom and I looked at each other like *whaaat*! That was never imaginable back home. We said *yes*—in unison—then laughed. The sales lady sat me at the demonstration bar in the middle of the store and grabbed the sample from the shelf. Mom stood across from me and occasionally walked back and forth around the store. Before the lady began, she asked me if it was okay to touch my hair. I said sure. As she began to work in the moisturizer, she started complimenting me on my hair.

"Can I just say, I love your hair," she said. "The tight curls, softness, and before getting halfway through it, the really good smells...what do you currently use?" she asked.

"Just some stuff from back home," Mom said.

"Well, I am just working in some moisturizer that helps to hydrate the scalp as well," she said.

"Oh my gosh, I wish my thin hair was this thick and luscious. I'm not hurting you, am I?" she asked.

"No," I said.

By this time, there were a few more people who had come into the store and were now watching the sales lady massage my big ol' curly afro. I could hear them as they walked up.

Oh my gosh, I love your hair. That is some really curly hair you have little lady. That must be a task to manage.

Mom said thank you to the comments. I just sat there. Mom told the sales lady that the product was showing a difference in my hair. Once she was all done and Mom thanked her for the trial, the lady just kept playing in my hair. I tried to slide out of the seat, but she followed me with every move. She just kept saying how soft-n-tight my curls were, and that it gave them even more personality and definition. Mom finally gave her a stern, *we're gonna continue our shopping and consider coming back to make a decision.* As we walked out of the store, the few customers remaining in the store paid me compliments on my hair. I, on the other hand, felt like the elephant that had left the room.

Once we were back at home, Mom put away leftovers; I played with my new bear, unpacked another box of my stuff, finished up some homework, and chilled until bedtime. As I got ready for my bedtime, I remembered Jordan—one of Sofie's friends—asked me about Girl Scouts. She gave me a handout with information on it. I was so glad Mom gave me some personal time to get myself together and do "me" in my new room. Now, I found a flyer that I had completely forgotten about. I rushed into Mom's room while she was on the phone with a friend from back home. I handed her the flyer and began talking to her while she was talking. She gave me the—*you kidding me*—look. I kept talking. Finally, she gave me a look while pointing to her phone, said *"busy,"* and shooed me out of her room. Once off the phone, she came in to get the paper. I told her I wanted to join and about some of the girls from my classes who did Girl Scouts. She just said *"we'll see"* and walked away.

Chapter 7

The first Girl Scout meeting was awkward but exciting. I finally began to show some of my class and schoolmates the true Ari. I even wore my hair naturally curly. To my surprise, the girls were acting friendlier than they did in school. The troop leader was Jordan's Aunt Missy. Jordan had told me a little bit about Missy at recess. She told me how she was super cool, stylish, loved to go places, and had two boys but spent lots of time with Jordan because she wanted a daughter *really* bad. When I met Aunt Missy, she was excited to meet me. Jordan told her I was from the "Chi." She told me about her visit to Chicago. She loved the city. Once she was done with the meeting's agenda,

Aunt Missy called the meeting to order and made me stand up before everyone to introduce myself. I was really glad I came—we made homemade ice cream. Once we were done with Girl Scout stuff, Aunt Missy allowed us to go hang out in her backyard as she prepared lunch for us. While outside, we sat on a blanket and ate our ice cream. One girl—Lucy—asked me why we moved from Chicago. I thought, oh goodness, here we go—*again*! I heard Mom, Aunt Winnie, and Naanah in the back of my head. They were telling me to be nice and friendly. I finished licking my spoon and took a small deep breath.

"We were tired of the snow," I said.

"Is it always snowing?" Jasmine asked.

This isn't 20-20, I thought to myself. Before, I could say anything, Sofie came to my defense. She told the girls to stop asking such dumb questions. It was ok; I didn't mind sharing. In my mind, I knew it was the only way we would ever become friends. The girls went on to ask me a few more questions. Finally, we got to what I think they *really* wanted to know.

"How do you get your hair to be curly one day then straight like mine the next?" Anna asked.

I was almost annoyed, but if I didn't educate them, they would be—as Aunt Winnie said—*ignorant* (ig-no-rant) *forever.*

"My hair is naturally curly and has been this way since birth. My mom says I had a head full of curly black hair when I was born, and it's been that way ever since," I explained. "It takes a lot to keep up because, as you can see, I'm black."

We all laughed.

"I sweat a lot, have to keep it moisturized since the sun is always on it, and I have to use stuff to keep it from getting twisted up together. When my hair is straight, I wash it about three or four times; it depends on how dirty my hair is," I said. "I probably use different hair stuff than you all. My mom uses some stuff our beautician gave her to make it silky and straight for about two weeks. My momma blow dries and flat irons it. This was just black girl hair 101."

They all sat very attentively. In the midst of earning black girl hair knowledge street credit—LOL—some asked to touch it. I let them touch, smell, and even rub it against their face.

"Lunch is ready, ladies," Aunt Missy said.

We all ran in for lunch at the same time. At the end of girl scouts, we all stood in a circle, said the pledge, and gave each other a hug. Parents started filing in to collect their kids. A few of the girls even said they were really glad I came and decided to join the troop.

Girl Scouts actually ended up being one of the best decisions made so far. I was able to experience camping outdoors, an overnight stay at a water park and resort, meeting more—and more—girls, and *we participated in a town parade!* I would not have imagined doing that back home. Back at school, I collected a few more friends. Arizona did not feel so bad. I still had my calendar marked for when we were jet setting back home for summer vacation.

Chapter 8

Summer vacation *finally* arrived. I was extremely happy to be going back home. Mom and I sat at the computer together looking for flights back home. It seemed like hours had passed. I just gave up and went to bed out of pure exhaustion and frustration. I was so excited when Mom finalized our travel plans. My bags were packed two weeks before it was time to head to the airport. Mom was right...once we arrived back home, everyone was excited to see us. The Fave, Aunt Shonnie, picked us up from the airport. The minute she got out of her truck, she was screaming and squeezing—and screaming and squeezing. It hurt a little but felt good at the same time. Azzi screamed

Mom's name so loud. As they hugged each other, everyone at the airport turned around and smiled at them. Before getting into the truck, I took a deep breath. I let all the smells of home fill up my lungs. I swear, Aunt Shonnie talked all the way to Naanah's house—where we were staying. It sounded like she was talking how she was driving—fast. As I gazed out of her window in awe at how bright the city lights were, I faded in and out of the conversation that Mom and Aunt Shonnie were having. My eyes welcomed the familiar sights of home. It seemed like she asked me a ton of questions.

How you like it?

How's school?

What are your new friends like?

What do they wear, niecy-pooh?

How do they talk?

Was anyone mean?

How is your room decorated?

It seemed to go on and on—and on. She told us that she needed to stop by her house and pick up my cousins; *they were dying to see us.*

She didn't know, but I was feeling the same way. There is nothing like family. I learned that—it seemed like—the hard way.

Once we made it to pick up Jaya, Cordi, and Nate, we headed towards Naanah's house. As soon as my cousins made it out to the truck, Jaya began screaming and hugging me super hard.

"HEYYYYYYYY, ARIIIIIIIII," Jaya screamed. "I missed you so much!"

I just hugged her back and smiled. To hear that she missed me as much as I missed her made me feel *really* good. I thought to myself, we have *so* much catching up to do. I can't wait to tell her about school and how I had to get all "ghetto" on them. As we pulled up to Naanah's house, I could not tell if anyone was home or not. I didn't even see Aunt El's truck parked out front. My heart sank. I just knew everybody would be waiting for us.

Cordi and Azzi grabbed our bags from the back. We all headed inside. I could smell food.

"Smmmmmmmmmmmmmmm ahhhhhh," I said. "I missed that smell. Somebody must have been to Tony's Vienna because the scent seemed to be fresh in the air."

I opened up the second door.

"*Surprise!*" *all* of my family yelled.

Everybody in my entire family was there! I felt so loved, missed, and like I wanted to cry! I think I actually did drop a side tear. I hugged everybody in the room. I couldn't see Mom's face, but I am sure she was surprised—just like I was—to see *everybody* there.

We put our bags up in the guest bedroom and headed back down to the party. We talked, laughed, and ate for—what seemed like—hours. Mom told everybody how I was scaring everybody when I went all "Chi-town hood." I was embarrassed but supported at the same time.

"That's right, Ari. Show them you ain't a punk," Cousin Frank said.

I talked to Aunt El about how the boys teased me about my hair when I wore it Natural. Aunt El wears her hair natural too; I knew she would definitely understand how I felt. She gave me the hardest hug ever and told me to do *me*, be *proud* of ME. Don't let anyone talk crazy to me about my hair. It is *beautiful*, *I am* BEAUTIFUL. If they have an issue with it, it's *their* loss. Aunt El really knew what to say to make me smile. As we focused back in on the rest of the family, Aunt

Winnie and Naanah were telling everyone about their visit, shopping, and the weather. It felt like we were up forever before everyone left and we called it a night. Jaya and Azzi stayed with us. Cordi and Nate left with Aunt Shonnie. She kept telling us we needed to get some rest and to be on time for brunch. Man, it felt *good*—to be home!

While at home for summer break, Mom and I both made sure to see our regular beautician, Aunt Cat, to get our hair treated before we returned home. Mom and Aunt Cat have been friends since I was three years old. Aunt Cat is the only person, besides herself, Mom will allow to do anything to my hair. If you didn't know Aunt Cat was happy to see us, her screams of joy sure said it all. She hugged me crazy tight. It felt good. She immediately got the water ready to wash and style my hair. As she washed my hair and combed through the conditioner, she asked me lots of questions about my school, new friends, the weather, the food, the flight, and finally my hair. I told Aunt Cat about the names some of the kids called me when I wore my hair natural. Based on her reactions, either she was truly shocked or a really good actress. I asked her for advice on making my curls look shinier and staying put when it's extremely hot outside. She gave me a bag of hair maintenance products for sun protection, my curls, and scalp.

"Child, your hair is *gorgeous*; I bet they won't be talking trash NAH," she said.

We both laughed. I leaned in toward the mirror and ran my fingers through my butter silk and satiny straight hair. I also asked Mom if Aunt Cat could cut me some bangs—to give me a different look. Aunt Cat and Mom approved. As I sat and waited for Mom to finish up, all of the other clients–coming and going— complimented my hair. A few even asked me if *all* of it was mine. I sat with my chin high, in pride, and said *yup*. I felt *so* beautiful. When I wear my hair natural, sometimes, I don't feel as beautiful and confident. I feel like it makes me stand out and become the center of— unwanted—attention.

Chapter 9

My returns to Arizona from summer breaks, up until the sixth grade, went pretty uneventfully—school, Girl Scouts, and exploring Arizona on the weekends. Mom made sure to tell me every day to have a good day and—on my natural days—that she loved my hair. My fellow Girl Scout troop members were my new crew of friends, except one or two. *This did get better*, I thought while sitting in the finale of fifth grade promotion ceremony. I was super excited about moving on to middle school. New kids, new courses, better cafeteria food, and a new wardrobe! Woohoo! By middle school, I managed to rustle up a few black friends along the way. As usual, the very first moment in middle school, I switched my hair from straight to curly, the questions came flooding in. That time, however, I was not so annoyed.

At Miles Middle School, there were a few other kids who wore their hair curly one week, then straight and down their backs the next—including different colors and styles. Many of the girls wore extensions in their hair when they had a different look. I loved being surprised at the new looks my friends, peers, and even enemies returned back to campus with—after the weekends. It made me feel like I belonged and was not the main attraction animal. This time around, when questioned about my mane, I simply educated the inquisitive (n qui zi tive) on my hair being mine and 100% natural. Frequently, their response was simply...*oooh* or *OMG; you are so lucky that is your natural hair!* Some of the boys complimented me on my hairstyles—regardless if it was straight and silky or wild and curly. I appreciated those compliments. It let me and my self-esteem know we were not the ugly ducklings on campus, LOL.

The boys who were still being butt heads made it their silly business to tease me about my hair. Some days it was easy to ignore them when I felt inside that I was beautiful. Other days, it really hurt my feelings and made me question everything about me. It was very frustrating to hear the silly, mean, and stupid comments made. I just *really* wished they would grow up and accept me for *me*. I began avoiding activities on campus, school dances, and hanging out with school friends—for fear of being teased. It wasn't a bully situation. It was just silly kids being *very immature*.

"Ari, are you ready for dinner?" Mom asked.

My thoughts were interrupted—*again*.

"Almost," I shouted.

Because middle school was full of kids from *everywhere*, with all types of issues, hair was not a big deal—beyond that silly crew. There were a lot more of us "Mocha" people, as I like to be called, running around campus. It created a more accepting culture. Many of us black girls on campus wore natural curls, afros, weaves, braids, wigs (YUP wigs) and perms. In fact, the only girls who alternated (all-ter-nate-d) their hairstyles in the middle of the week, like I did, were either Mexican or Mixed. I'm not saying I was the only Black girl who had naturally curly hair, but there were only two other girls in my class—on my side of campus.

Seventh grade year, we started a club called *Locs of Love*. We would get together once a month, share crazy stories about our hair, people, boys, and hair care management. We would often have serious discussions when someone encountered a situation where we were made to feel less than pretty. It seemed as if all of us were a work in progress when it came to accepting our uniqueness. *L.O.L.'s* would share hair care secrets, samples, styles, and even have a guest speaker come to share with us. It felt amazing to finally have a safe haven to turn to when Mom was not around. We even got together to watch *BET's Black Girls Rock* awards show. It felt empowering to know that there were millions of others just like me—proud to be just like me.

While in *L.O.L.,* I learned I was dealing with—what they called—low self-esteem and shame issues. Our Language Arts teacher, Ms. Jackson, brought a clinical family therapist to one of our sessions. We were able to share some *really* personal experiences, feelings, and situations about being black and biracial girls living in Arizona. At one point, it was so moving, even Ms. Jackson needed the box of tissues. The therapist suggested for us to be trans-, trans-parent or completely open about how we felt—good or bad. She provided us with information about self-esteem and told us about organizations outside of school we could join to spread knowledge, support, and *love*. We also wrote a letter to our parents. We told them about the worst experience we have had—so far—because of our uniqueness and explained how we turned that bad experience into something good. We also thanked them for their support and *love*. To show our unity and support for one another, we all wore pearls and a pair of Afro-puff girl earrings—sent by Aunt El—during eighth grade promotion ceremony. It was important for us as Black Natural girls, who also *rock*, to show our sisterhood, support, and love for who we are. Now, when I decide to go natural, instead of straight, I feel good and happy about it. I am *L.O.L. forever*, and I am literally laughing out loud—knowing I have conquered such a huge issue in my life.

Chapter 10

Looking back on what seemed like forever, I packed to head home for a two week visit—instead of the entire summer break. This visit would be special. No one knew I got my driver's license. Mom and I decided to keep it a secret and surprise everyone. As the night set and the lights in the house went off, I continued to pack. Finally, satisfied with my packing, room cleaning, and airplane outfit, I called it a night.

I was awakened by bright iridescent lights shining in my face. The lights were so bright; I thought I was going blind for a second. *Come on let's get up... can't be late.* I continued to lie—cozy—in my bed. I knew what was coming next but was too blinded by drowsiness to prevent it. The covers were ripped off. My body was exposed to the cool morning air.

"Get up... let's go," Mom said.

She hastily walked out of the room.

"I'm up... I'm up," I groaned.

We don't want to be late for the conference or the airport. Before we boarded our Saturday evening flight back home, I was headed to be on a very special panel to speak to a group of girls, who recently relocated from Chicago to Arizona. We would speak about Natural hair care, self-esteem, and adapting to new environments. I was really excited and nervous at the same time. I had never done anything like it before. However, our beautician, Tina, whom Mom and I finally found out here in Arizona, reassured me I would do an *amazing* job.

The conference is at a youth center near Tina's salon. Mom and Tina thought I would be a great role model with lots of encouraging information to share with young, Black Natural girls because of the challenges I had with moving, adjusting to a new school, making new friends, experiencing new adventures, creating a new life, and finding a hairstyle and stylist who could handle my hair. As a successful survivor of it all, I liked the idea of making someone else have an easier transition than I did.

Once we got to the conference center, I took a deep breath and looked around at all the work that was put into it. *Wow.* I didn't want to admit it out loud, but it was amazing. My mom guided me to the area where everyone on the panel would be sitting, told me to knock'em dead, and be myself. I had also invited the L.O.L's to come out to the conference. As I looked out on the growing audience of mostly young Black girls, they all had different hairstyles, shades of Black Beauty, and sizes. I saw my girls seated all together with their afro-puffs dangling in their ears. They were waving at me. I waved back and mouthed, *"Crazy right?"* The girls continued to file in for another 10-15 minutes. The panel of speakers also started to take their seats next to me. Tina was the moderator. There were two other teen girls. One had braids, and the other had dread-locs with blonde and red tips. We spoke to each other and settled into our seats. There was a Black, female family therapist on the panel, a local high school basketball player, a single mom, and— surprisingly—a single Dad.

Tina calmed everyone down with a greeting and acknowledgement of our session beginning. She introduced everyone on the panel. She also had the Black girls, young and old alike, stand and recite an empowerment slogan. We immediately jumped into the session. Everyone had notecards prepared on what they were going to say. I, on the other hand, thought being my naturally silly and informative self would be just fine. I glared into the audience, thinking to myself, *I got this.* More and more started to come in. As they continued to pour into the room, my heart began to beat faster and faster. I guess I had a really weird look or something; the girl next to me asked if I was okay.

This time, I was glad someone interrupted my thoughts—on my racing heart and shaking hands, LOL.

"Hmm," I managed to mumble out of my now dry mouth.

"Oh, yeah...a little nervous. Did you know all these girls would be here?" I asked.

"I knew there would be some but not *this many*," she said. "They comin in here like a herd of cattle."

We both laughed. That made it a lot easier to take a sip from the cup of water sitting in front of me.

At the last minute, I decided to split my hair down the middle and wet part of it. It would be naturally curly. It was weird but *totally* worked and captured the audience's attention. As I spoke, I took the pitcher of water before me and wet the other side of my hair. At first, people started to gasp at what they were witnessing. I smiled, paused, and explained a metaphor of perceptions, looks, and comments affecting young girls who are already dealing with so much as a Minority. I talked about being from Chicago, my life experiences, and how things changed—not all in a good way. I answered a few questions from the little girls who were 12-years-old and younger. Before I finished, I acknowledged my support system—the L.O.L.'s. Once I was done and back in my seat, everyone clapped and cheered. For the first time, in a very long time, I felt genuinely *happy* about being in Arizona. This experience would have never happened back home. We finished up the conference, greeted a few people, and extended a few hugs—to girls who shared some really heart provoking stories about being teased and even bullied because of their hair. Lastly, we made our way to the airport to catch our flight home.

Chapter 11

I sat in the shampoo bowl to get my hair washed.

"Welcome home, Ari," said Aunt Cat.

"Where's your Mom," she asked.

"She's back at Naanah's," I said.

Aunt Cat immediately turned the water off and looked at me in concern.

"Well, how did you get here?" she inquired.

"I drove," I voiced.

"*Shut the front door*," she said. "Child, you is *driving*. *Lord*, I am getting old."

We both laughed.

"So, little Ms. License, what are we doing with this hair?" she asked.

"I actually just want a wash and natural style and—of course—extra products to use when I get back home," I said.

"So, we are going to wear the natural curls and not straighten this luscious thick head of hair?! A*lrighty* then," she said. "Things are definitely changing for the good out there in Arizona." She had a huge smile.

The water was now on. We caught up on everything going on at home. I told Aunt Cat about the L.O.L.'s and the Young Black and Confident Conference. We talked about my presentation and the impact it had on those who were there. Aunt Cat, who is also natural but rocks braids and a wig from time to time, expressed how proud she was of me for embracing my true, God-given beauty. The trip to the salon was no different than any other trip. I received a lot of compliments and questions of authenticity (aww-then-tis-city).

When we arrived at Naanah's house, everyone was asleep. Because our flight would be arriving so late, we picked up a rental car this time around. My arrivals home are more-so expected than anticipated. It has become the new norm in my life, LOL. Everyone patiently... still with excitement... waits until I arrive, instead of anticipating my arrival. When I walked in the house from Aunt Cat's salon, I looked up to find everyone standing under a banner. It read "Congratulations, Ari!" It turns out, Mom—sneaky-squirrel, again—organized a family party to celebrate all of my accomplishments and growth. There were no physical gifts. However, there were a lot of gifts for the soul. Everyone joked about how they would have to hide their keys from now on. They told stories of learning to drive, taking the test, and getting their first car. Mom also made everyone stop and be quiet when she gave a toast to my performance at the YBC Conference. Traveling back home was still exciting because I *love* to travel. However, I am now starting to understand some of the reasons why Mom decided, back on that cold winter day, to deliver—what was just—the most horrific news ever. Being able to take on new challenges, experience a different way of life, and learn more about yourself as you grow, are lessons I can use as I continue to get older. Being pushed outside my—CHI-TOWN—comfort zone has made me a somewhat smarter and happier person—so far.

Chapter 12

Even though I confidently wear my hair in what-so-ever style I choose, my freshman year of high school—like my very first day at Rancho—was not the proper time to introduce the "Afro." Even with *so* many people proudly rockin' natural styles and white people wearing big hair—a.k.a. their version of an afro—I still was not ready to put myself on display. I wanted to become comfortable with, yet again, being the new Black girl on the block. This time, I would be in a sea of hundreds of students and the teachers. Contrary (kon-tray-ree) to what you may think, people judge from the outside in—and what is trending on the internet. Before I left to begin brand new high school experiences, I put on the mask of conformity, not individuality (in-di-vid-u-al-itee). Mom reluctantly allowed me to go see Aunt Cat one last time to get my hair done—before we planned our return.

My new high school, Rich Mountain North, was a school where the curriculum was college-focused and challenging, there were a variety of language courses, high test scores, and lots of extra-curricular opportunities—in case I wanted to shoot for a sports scholarship. Unfortunately, *none* of my middle school or Girl Scout buddies were going to be there. All of my friends were going to the neighborhood high schools—*together*.

"Here I go, *again*!" I thought.

Mom delivered the news one month before graduation.

"Sooooo, Ari, to make sure you get the best high school experience with lots of rigor (rig-or) and opportunity, plus two years of Spanish and French, we will be researching these ten schools over the summer," she said.

"Are you kidding me," I exclaimed. "I am going to have to live 'Rancho' all over again."

"I understand. I promised you things would get better. They did," she said. "Look at you—wearing your hair curly, holding your head up high, and taking on new adventures. This will be no different."

I just sighed out of exhaustion and disbelief. I just knew I would be able to tackle a new school, new stresses, and the new changes being a high school teenager would throw at me. NOPE!

"This behavior of Mom's is really starting to become a pattern," I considered. "Well, here I go again. Hopefully, this time around, making friends, the cafeteria food, and the whole nine will be *much* smoother than Rancho. Here goes nothing, Ari."

Chapter 13

My cellphone interrupted my session of i-spy. Destiny, from the *LOC's,* was on my—soon-to-be—new high school stomping grounds. She was inviting me to hangout before we all ventured off to our new lives. Her mom setup a special luncheon for us in the backyard. We dressed like we were going to a special summertime affair—dresses, our pearls, dressy shoes, and our natural do's. I was really looking forward to seeing those girls *one last* time. Who knew what would happen over the next four years. One last—lasting—moment would be just the cup of booster that I needed.

"Sounds great, I can't wait...I'll see you soon," I concluded.

She gave me all the information and a little gossip tea on the side. I immediately informed my mother of my invitation to gain approval, checked her calendar of events, and started my campaign of "I needs." LOL. My "I needs" campaign was all the things *I thought* I would need from the mall to look *fabulous*—for any occasion. As I rattled down the list of "I needs," I talked to my Mom about it. She just rolled her eyes and continued reading her book.

"Once you decide how you want your hair, we can discuss the rest," Mom said.

"We have to wear our hair natural," I said. "Also, we can only wear lip gloss."

"Well, in that case, this should only take you a week to get yourself together," Mom joked.

We both laughed.

"*Oh*, you have to come!" I said.

I think I saw her eyes roll past me. I walked into my room and began tearing up my closet—searching for my look.

Chapter 14

Destiny's Mom really turned the event into a mini production. We pulled up to the valet stand at the end of their driveway. Music was playing; it was John Legend. Mom and I were escorted out of our seats. There were rose petals along the side of the house. The backyard was *beautiful!* Destiny's Mom *really* did her *thang*. She turned our hangout into something magical. There was a white tent with lights hanging from it. Mason jars were filled with water and floating candles. Name cards on round tables were in the front in Tiffany blue. It had pearl white place settings. The chairs even matched. When I walked completely inside the backyard, I think my eyes jumped out of my head. I'm telling you, my mouth stayed wide open. A waiter offered me a beverage in a really cute champagne glass—it was punch of course, LOL. Once I was finished being overwhelmed by the decorations, I found the girls—just as Mom was about to interrupt my *thoughts*, LOL.

I ran over to Destiny and the crew. We began screaming, talking all at once, complimenting one another, modeling for one another, and looking for those who were late arrivals. Destiny told us that her Mom *insisted* on having an "over the top" party for *us*. She said her Mom, who is originally from Indiana, wanted us to experience some "Black girls' *Rites of Passage*"—Destiny's words...not mine—before splitting up for high school. We all agreed. Whatever the reason was, we *loved it*.

As I stood in the midst of the constant chatter, I noticed there was a special table in the center. There was a small box on the table and little bags in our seats. My thoughts were interrupted—blank stare. This time it was Destiny's Mom. She had a microphone and was walking and talking throughout the backyard.

"If you can hear me...please take your seats," she said. "If you can hear me...please take your seats."

She's a teacher. She used the teacher "soft" call, hahahaha. Once everyone was focused in on her, standing or from their seats, she requested for all of us— L.O.L.'s—to join her in the center of the yard. She presented us by our *full* Birth Certificate names, *okay*. We were presented with a salutation of "Miss" in the beginning. As she called for us, she went to each seat.

As she called our names, different boys—some from school and others...well, I had no clue—took us each by the arm and properly seated us. Once we were all seated, they disappeared—it seemed. Mrs. Johnson asked everyone to take their seats. She stood before us, smiling. The minute we were all seated, you know we started peeping through our goodie-bags and investigating the special boxes on the table. That moment was abruptly interrupted by Mrs. Johnson's slightly elevated tone. She began with her explanation of our requested attendance. She wanted to personally take the time out to provide us—young girls—with an evening of elegance, encouragement, empowerment, and celebration. She was appreciative that we all "organically" came together to create a support system that celebrates our race, culture, heritage, success, and— most of all—*natural beauty.*

That evening was just one way to introduce us to the world as budding, young, talented, intelligent, and *beautiful black* young ladies. The people clapped and whistled so loudly. I swear the neighbors heard it several blocks away. She asked us to turn our attention to the screen for a brief presentation. It was set up behind us at the far end of the yard. We all looked at each other.

This better not be some old embarrassing moments from school. Omg, what is this? Oh, dear Lord, what are we gonna watch? My mom's face appeared! My eyes bucked out of my face, LOL.

"Wait...when did this happen? She didn't say anything," I voiced. "SHHHHHHH, SHHHHHH...I need to hear."

"Is this thing on?" she asked.

She was tapping the mic on the collar of her blouse and making a crazy funny face. We all started laughing at it.

She cleared her throat and began with a great big old exhale.

She pulled out some of my pink and purple notepad paper that sits on my desk. I recognized the paper because I use it whenever I write letters to my friends and family back home—in the Chi.

"Who told her to use my stuff?" I thought.

She began to read a letter, *to me*, through the video. She talked about all of my accomplishments—from the moment we knew we were gonna make the move. She used funny situations and jokes to talk about moments when I was not the best person to be around because I was sad and missing home. She was proud of me for *accepting what was divinely in order*. When I think about it, I did make some pretty special and spectacular friends and connections. She wished me well. Before her presentation was over, she looked into the camera, wiped her face full of tears, and said one final thing. *You is kind. You is smart. You is important.* We all laughed so hard—in unison. Now you see why *I am so silly*! She closed her tribute with words of encouragement. They were about always accepting, loving, and walking in the *person* that God fearlessly designed me to be. *Own it till infinity.* Everyone clapped, whistled, and snapped at her tribute. We all received one tribute after another—with the erupting applause. For a moment, everyone was using their table napkins to wipe their eyes.

After the video presentations were done, we turned our attention back up to the front of the tent.

Mrs. Johnson was encouraging everyone to give us a round of applause.

We all stood. Some of us were "Miss America" waving to the crowd, some of us fiddling with our dress hems, and some of us gripping the back of the chair. It felt like we were a bunch of misfits who were uncomfortable with *all of* the attention. Finally, we were allowed to be seated.

"We just wanted to celebrate you as future *black leaders* of tomorrow, encourage and uplift your spirits, and send you off to high school feeling like the *fabulous* budding *greats* that you are. Enjoy yourselves tonight because you earned it," said Mrs. Johnson.

Once finished, she—and all the Moms—came over to give each and every one of us a big hug. We also received a rose in our favorite color.

"Mom, how did you...when did you...you didn't tell me, *really*?" I questioned.

"Sweetie, I don't have to tell you *everything*!" she replied.

She smiled and hugged me one last time before taking her seat.

"One more thing, ladies," Mrs. Johnson said. "As members of the Locs of Love Club, you will find a few special keepsakes, tide-bonding treasures, and the entire letter that I championed your Moms to write—for this occasion—in your bags."

Let's get this par-tey started. Dinner services will begin.

We each tried to hold off dumping out our bags. It was hard but we encouraged each of us to wait. Besides, as soon as that mic went off, food started coming left and right.

Mrs. Johnson had a special soul food chef come in and make a meal that made you wanna slap *big momma*, LOL. After we finished our soup, salad, and full Sunday dinner meal, a big beautiful cake came through the crowd with sparkles going off. It had each of our lil bodies poised at the bottom. I swear it looked like something seen on a cake baking competition. I could not wait to tear into it. Before cutting the cake, we took individual and group pictures. We used our printable Polaroid cameras from our bags— *whaaat*! The cake was *delicious*. We went from R&B music straight to club hits. Some people, who began to mix and mingle around, were removed. A dance floor appeared out of *nowhere*!

I don't know who hit the floor first, but before I knew it, we were on it—getting our groove on! As we continued to party the night away, I felt a tap on my shoulder. I turned around to see that it was three of the girls from the YBC conference. We all screamed with our hands waving in the air. People slowed down—just enough—to make sure everything was okay. It was exciting.

"Hey," I said. I gave them all big hugs. "You all look so good," I told them. I ushered them off the— crowded and loud—dance floor and over to the side. "Are you guys excited? What did you think of the conference?" I asked. "Wasn't that the best thing ever? Isn't this the *Best Thing Ever?*" I dabbed my face and forehead with an oil lifter from my clutch purse.

"*Yass!*" they said in unison.

We all laughed.

Several girls at the party and from the YBC would be attending our Middle School—taking over the duties of L.O.L. That was great. We knew it would be in good hands with those new members. In between hugs from other guest at the party, Destiny and I continued to talk with the girls. As the girls headed toward the dance floor—to do the bus stop dance—Destiny and I noticed another special guest in the crowd. It was Ms. Jackson. She was *dolled up* and *snatched to capacity!* She looked so young and different—like a real *woman...not* a *teacher.* She told us that she agreed with all of the fabulous words spoken about us all evening. She ushered herself over to the dance floor to get her groove on, too. We ended the night shortly after 3 a.m. Mom and I were among the last to leave. I walked to the car barefoot and danced *out* of my shoes. I was not ashamed either.

"Best night ever," I told my mom.

She just laughed, tapped my arm, and opened my door for me to get in the car.

Chapter 15

My bed was *completely* covered with all of my new school clothes. My floor was *completely* covered with all of my new school supplies. My hair had been all over my head for two weeks. It was super—crazy—hot and icky. Getting ready for my first day of school was turning out to be more stressful than I anticipated. Lying in the middle of the floor, I thought to myself.

What do I wear?

Gosh, how hot is it going to be?

Do I wear Chucks, Vans, or sandals?

I just gave up and gave in to the sleep.

"Ari, are you ready?" a voice said. "Ari, ARE you READY?"

Am I ready for what? I rolled over on a pack of pens. Mom was standing at my door. She looked very irritated.

"Your room is a *mess*! What has been going on in here?" Mom inquired.

"What? Huh? Um...I was just getting stuff together and fell asleep. Imma clean it up...don't worry!" I replied. "Is it time to go already?!"

"*No*, we have an hour before we have to leave for the freshman mixer," she said "You betta get your... *Get up* and get this mess cleaned up!"

She stormed away from me—and my storm— and slammed the door on her way out. By the time Mom came back, it was just about cleaned up. She peeked into my room and told me to be ready in ten minutes. I simply said ok and put my last pair of Hollister jeans in my closet. I immediately closed the closet door—which is also a full length mirror—and check my outfit for the mixer. I decided to switch from shorts to distressed jeans and a layered tank look.

'What am I going to do with my hair?" I mumbled.

I could choose a ponytail. Or I could have it down and wild, up in a bun, back with a headband, or a part down the middle—with two large bantu knots in the back.

"Five minutes, Ari," Mom said. "You don't want to be late."

"*Okay*," I replied. "Do I really need to go to this stupid thing?" I grumbled. "UGH, this stupid hot hair makes me sick. I should just cut it all off."

Mom came to my room.

"Ari, are you—"

"Do we have time to flat iron my hair?" I asked. I looked up at her with tears in my eyes.

"*Um...no!*" she said. She had a stern frown on her face. "Ari, it is a mixer, not the first day of school," she said. "It is a billion degrees outside—too hot to wear your hair down any kind of way." She knelt down behind me with the brush, the can of sculpting mousse, a headband, and a ponytail holder. "I know you don't want to go. I know you don't know anybody. I know you are blaming me for *another* change in your life. I will accept that," she stated. "Work to understand how this will be one of the best decisions and changes made for you ever. *Trust me!*"

I didn't say anything. She just continued fixing my hair. I wiped my face and put on my earrings. By the time she was done, I was content (kon-tent) with what she produced—making me look somewhat pretty. My hair was neatly brushed into a well tucked bun. My headband held my loose hair down and off my edges. My sideburns were neatly laid along my ears. I looked left then right. I approved.

"Thanks," I said.

I didn't respond to what Mom said while fixing my hair. I just prepared myself for one the most awkward moments in my—high school—life. I gathered my phone, ear buds, and purse then followed Mom out the door.

Chapter 16

Even though I agreed to go to the mixer, I didn't think it would be any fun. I didn't know anyone. Everyone there would know someone. It was such a waste of money and time. As we pulled up to the campus, there were signs stating: FRESHMAN MIXER DROP OFF HERE. We pulled up behind the line of cars. One after another, kids were being dropped off.

"Here I go," I voiced.

I paused to look at Mom. It was a *please don't make me do this* look.

"Honey, you look super cute. You will have a good time," she said. "Text me when you are ready. I'm gonna meet Destiny's Mom nearby."

"Ok," I replied.

I headed on to the campus with the other kids. As I walked, I noticed kids running up to one another. They were so excitement about seeing one another. Guys were giving each other dap handshakes. I was *Lonely Lilly*. I considered looking for somewhere to hide until it was time to go. I got closer to the gym, thanks to the large colored arrows painted on the ground. I heard the music playing. Ok, so they were *Pandora-ing* the latest music...so what? *Wrong*, there was a live DJ from HOT JOINTS 101.3 JAMZ. A bit impressed, I smirked.

I got to the check in area and was immediately greeted by a girl with big curly hair. Her shirt read: Greeter. She pointed me to the sign-in table, gave me a bottle of water, and a granola bar. I walked inside and found a corner to scope out the masses. Kids were bunched in groups throughout the huge gymnasium. At the far end, there was a familiar voice projecting through the speaker. It shocked the bejesus out of me. The girls next to me said I shook and let out a loud sound. We started laughing.

"We did the same thing," one of the girls said. She leaned forward and looked at my name tag. "A-rye...is that how you pronounce your name?" she asked.

I cupped my hand in the corner of my mouth—near her ear.

"No," I said. "It is ARE-REE." I showed her with my cellphone keypad.

"OMG, I am so sorry. I'm Renee," she said. "This is Jenee, my twin. We just moved here from Michigan,"

"I'm from Chicago," I stated.

"Yasss, we love Chicago!!!" they both said.

For the rest of the evening, we walked around together, sang to some of the same hits, and pointed out some of the cute boys in the room. The DJ must have gotten a request for country music. He went *Old Country* on us—for about thirty minutes. The three of us stepped outside to cool off, grab something to drink, and wait for the O.K. CORRAL to end, LOL. While we were out in the hall, we chatted about how we ended up in Arizona. We all missed home. Jenee was wearing Poetic Justice braids. Renee was wearing a long— model like— ponytail. I felt my bun starting to unravel from all the dancing and suggested we head to the bathroom.

Not only was I right, but I looked like an oily slice of pizza—from all the sweat on my face. Before fixing my hair, I took out a blotch swab to dab my face. Renee asked for one as well. I pulled out my brush and unraveled my bun.

"Girl, is that all *yo hur*?" Jenee asked. She had so much excitement. It kind of scared me.

"Um...yeah," I said.

"What are you, a *mutt?*" she asked.

"*What?*" I asked. "Wait, did you just ask me if I am a dog?"

"No, silly, I'm basically asking if you are mixed with something—all that good *white* girl curly hair, LOL," she said.

"Awww... naw, it's all *Negro* here, girl," I said. "I'm just blessed with some good hair, LOL."

"Lucky you," she followed-up.

I finished fixing my bun, clearing my face, applying a fresh coat of lip gloss, and we headed out the door—back into the gym. The bathroom was empty when we went in. By the time we were ready to leave, it was packed. The gym was unusually quiet. We agreed to head inside to see what was going on. Inside the gym, everyone was facing the stage.

"Ya'll, what if *my man Drake* came on stage!" Renee said.

Simultaneously, we all just started talking about what we would do. Our dream session quickly ended. A woman with red hair came on to the stage and commanded our attention. It turned out it was our Assistant Principal, Dr. Waters. Dr. Waters made us introduce ourselves to the people around us. She welcomed us to campus, promised she would be quick, encouraged us to get involved, and to have a wonderful first year. As she left the stage, we lightly applauded. Next, a student committee member came on the stage and explained the different club tables—assembled out on the football field. As Jenee, Renee, and I stood together, we checked out the people around us.

All of sudden—as Jenee was pointing out a *really* cute boy—we started being moved by the crowd. We went out of the door and onto the football field. I had never been on a football field in my life. I was pretty excited but concerned that it was still a bit too hot outside. I was not in for the drama of my hair curling up around my edges—looking a hot mess. It was just about time for the event to end. We walked around the field and looked at the different clubs, sports, and activities offered. We paused to exchange our cell phone numbers—to keep in touch once school started. The scoreboard on the field had a timer set for fifteen minutes. I texted Mom that I would be ready for a pickup in fifteen minutes—at the same drop off spot. As I said goodbye to Renee and Jenee, I noticed—walking to my pickup spot—there were signs: FRESHMAN MIXER PICKUP HERE. Cars, mini vans, motorcycles, and a small school bus were waiting in line for kids to come out.

I spotted Mom and hopped in the car.

"So, how was it?" she asked.

"It was good," I replied. "I am really glad I went. I ended up having a good time and met two people—twin sisters."

"See, I told you! You have to trust me," she said.

"You ever heard of a Mutt?" I asked.

"You mean like a dog?" Mom responded.

"No, a mixed person," I said.

"Umm...yeah, why?" she asked.

"Well, one of the twins asked me if I was a *mutt* when I unraveled my hair in the bathroom," I said.

"What did you say?" Mom asked.

"I said *no*. They basically said it was someone who was mixed," I replied.

"Well, how did that make you feel?" Mom asked.

"I mean...I thought I was being called a bad word," I said. "Once they explained it to me, I felt a little weird. I am starting to get use to people assuming I am not Black—once they see my hair. I saw a few kids with various kinds of hairstyles. They were wild in comparison to mine. Hopefully, this *will not* turn into Girl Scouts all over again."

It was quiet for a little while as we drove. I thought about my night. It was cool meeting "the twins." I also wished my—Black girl—hair would never be the topic of a conversation again.

"Can we stop for a snack; I'm starving," I said.

Once we were home, I showered and added some conditioner to set in my hair—all weekend long. It would give my hair some super sheen for the first day of school. On Sunday, Mom was definitely going to straighten the madness out for me.

Chapter 17

Sunday's are our chill time. We prep for the week and complete all chores. As I cleaned up the new mess I had made in my room, my mind began to wonder. Not to mention, I also began singing the songs that I heard Mom playing from the CD that Aunt Trudy made for us—when we first moved to Arizona.

"Wow, it has been six years since we first played that CD. So much has changed," I voiced.

I passed grade school with A's and B's, was in Girl Scouts, went—*for real*—camping, had my own phone, was a frequent flyer, spoke at a conference, wasn't afraid to wear my hair natural, a junior in high school, *and I got my driver's license!* Who would have thought…it would happen in Arizona. I wondered about high school—what it would be like inside the classroom. I definitely don't want to appear like I learned nothing from Rancho. I'd be fine; my teachers were pretty tough on us.

I tried on almost everything in my closet. Next, it was time to get my hair done. I was back in the mirror, sizing up my Momma's skills—two hours, one blow dry, and a super hot flat iron later. Sometimes, she can be a little lazy and leave me with some puffy hair at my roots. This time, my gosh, *she nailed it!* I finally decided between three potential outfits—to be a part of the final morning selection process. Finally, it was lights out. School began at 7 a.m. and I was not one for early mornings. Before I headed to bed, however, I received several text messages from the twins. Super excited about keeping in touch, we texted back and forth about first day fits, hair, and a meet up spot to claim as our lunch table—if we were all split up. Having to get up when it was still blue-black outside is *not* an easy chore. That is when it is the coolest—good thing for us.

Immediately, I jumped out of bed, cranked on my music and hopped in the shower. After my thirty-minute double exfoliating scrub—and two threats from Mom—I was out of the bathroom. I chose to go with a skater striped dress, fresh chucks, and a jean jacket. While it may have been blazing outside, inside it was fit for a polar bear, LOL. I was cool as a cucumber. Once we were a block away from campus, my pits, scalp, and hands were sweaty; my mouth was drier than the Sahara Desert. *Oh no, Oh NO, OH NOOOOO...let me calm down.* Mom worked too hard on my hair for it to spaz out on me. It was the first day of school; I was nervous about classes, making friends, looking cute to the boys, and impressing the teachers. I hopped out the car.

"Have a good day," Mom said.

I found some shade to review my agenda for the day. Renee and Jenee ended up finding me.

As a group, we had two classes together. Jenee and I had an additional class—French. Renee and I shared homeroom. We were all so relieved.

"Wowwwww," Jenee said.

"What?" Renee asked. "What's wrong?"

"Look at you, Ms. Chicago," Jenee said. She flipped the back of my hair with her hands.

"Oh," I said. *Here we go,* I thought. "Well, I decided to wait a minute before going completely natural," I said. "You never know how people will react. You even called me a mutt, LOL."

"I apologize for that," Jenee said "All that curly hair caught me off guard. I see now."

We all laughed at the same time and began to head toward campus. I told "the twins" a bit about me moving to Arizona—the issues I had on my *very* first day of school in third grade. I also told them a bit about the L.O.L.'s from middle school and the YBC conference that we were planning.

"My bad, girl...I definitely don't want it to seem like I am making fun or am jealous of all that luscious hur, LOL," Jenee stated.

She moved her hands through my hair.

"It's cool," I said.

I'm better with handling it now. Instead of just—*bam*—throwing my natural hair onto people, I have to ween them into seeing it," I said.

"That was a bit deep, first thing in the morning. We Black Natural Sistahs have to stick together," said Renee. She put her "fight the power" fist up and swirled around.

As we familiarized ourselves with the buildings, the bell rang for us to head inside. We walked to class, and it sounded like the hustle and bustle of downtown— during rush hour. With schedule in hand, I moved from class to class. I was praying not to be late. As I walked out of my last class—before lunch—I heard similar sounds to the gymnasium during the freshman mixer.

"What is happening out here?" I asked Kennedy. She was also a freshman and in my Spanish class.

"I don't know, sounds like music," she replied. "That's too loud to be someone bumping their music from the parking lot."

"I know right," I added.

We picked up our pace to the cafeteria and busted out of the building double doors—to the outdoor eating area. We were bombarded with the blaring sound of music playing over the intercoms. Jenee, Renee, Kennedy, and I looked at one another and smiled.

"Hey, do you guys mind if I sit with you all?" asked Kennedy.

"Sure," we all said.

We found a spot near the concession stand. It was opposite of some of the boys we recognized from the mixer. Lunch was far from what I had experienced at Rancho and Miles'. There were tons of people all over the place—eating, sitting on the grass, walking back and forth to and from different buildings, and standing in all the different food and snack lines. I was definitely *not* prepared for this type of action. However, I sure was glad it was a better experience than previous years being the new Black girl on the block. There were all kinds of people at this school. There were all kinds of normal and extremely weird hairstyles. Not a single soul asked me about my hair. In fact, I got a lot of compliments on my look. That calmed my nerves and increased my confidence. We each took turns grabbing either lunch or a snack from whichever line was the shortest. To avoid not having anywhere to sit and to be able to get our people watch on, we decided not to all go at once.

The afternoon was not so smooth. I was late for my final class of the day—History. For some reason, I could not find the right building—and go to the bathroom—all before the three-minute bell rang. As I walked into class, my teacher, Mr. History, immediately bombarded me with questions about my tardiness. I was so embarrassed that I felt sweat trickle down my arm pits. Just as I had cleared my throat, two other students

had come into the classroom behind me. Mr. History—
that's really his real name—allowed us to take a seat. He
proceeded to give us a history lesson on why we should
never be late for class—especially his. Three rows from
the back, there was a seat on one of the side of the room.
I tucked my head, tightened the strap of my new Eddie
Bauer backpack, slid into the seat, and put my head in
my hands. I suddenly felt warm breath close to my neck.
It caused me to spring around with my elbow in self-
defense and hit the boy behind me.

"Sorry," I said.

"It's ok. I just wanted to let you know that he's
been badgering us too," he whispered.

"Oh...wow, are you sure you're ok?" I asked. I
tilted my head to get a better look at his nose. "Whoa,"
I thought. "He's a cutie."

I tried to focus on him saying he was "good." I
quickly turned back around in my seat to face the front.
The bell rang. We all filed out of the classroom—
flooding the hallways in a chaotic madness. I took my
time and got a better look at *cutie patootie*. I also wanted
to see if he would wait for me and possibly say
something else. Maybe he would pay me a compliment,
something that boys do to girls they think are cute. I got

nothing, except a few additional seconds in the classroom with Mr. History.

"Please be on time for classes from now on, Ms. Ari," Mr. History said.

Our campus is a tech campus. Students use iPads instead of books and teachers work on Mac Pros instead of desktops at work stations.

"Yes sir," I said. I tucked my head, ran my fingers down my hair to make sure it wasn't puffy, and walked swiftly out the door.

Chapter 18

Mom was waiting for me in the lot under a shade tree. I finally made my way out of the building and across the campus. Kennedy, Jenee, and Renee all rode the bus to school. I didn't get a chance to say bye to them before leaving campus. It was for the best. I didn't want to seem too needy or clingy—on the first day. Before I could even get my seatbelt on, Mom began drilling me with questions.

How was it?

How was class?

Where did you sit in class?

Who did you eat lunch with?

Do you have homework?

Did you see anyone from the mixer?

How were your teachers?

What did you eat for lunch?

...on and on and ON!

"Geez, lady, can I get in the car first?" I mumbled.

"Sorry, I just wanted to know how everything went on your first day in high school," she said.

I didn't respond right away. So much had occurred. I just wanted a few minutes to take it all in. Being bombarded with these questions was unexpected and something I really did not want to deal with at the moment. Riding home, I realized I had not eaten. I was tired from getting up so early and had a ton of work to do. It was just day one of high school.

"Mom, can we discuss my first day a bit later?" I said. "I am super tired, hungry and in need of a nap right about now."

"Sure, we can chat later," she said. "I didn't get a chance to go grocery shopping. What do you want for dinner?"

"It doesn't matter," I said.

As soon as I made it home, I made a b-line for the bathroom—followed up by grabbing a snack. That apple tasted like steak...well...maybe chicken; we stopped eating red meat. Once I devoured my apple, my body hit the pillow. I instantly sank into a deep sleep. I was awakened hours later by Mom's loud laughter and clinking pots. I found my phone underneath my covers, buzzing uncontrollably. There were fifteen text messages and a few missed calls.

"Man, how long was I sleeping?" I voiced.

It was 7:30 pm. I slept for *four hours*! I wobbled my way into the kitchen.

"Well, if it isn't our little freshman," Mom said.

She was talking on the phone.

"Who's that?" I asked.

"Aunt El and Aunt Shonnie," she replied. "They asked how your first day of high school went."

"It was good," I replied.

Mom passed me her phone to speak with my Aunts. Just like Mom, they asked me a ton of questions. This time, I was in the mood to answer without hesitation. We talked about the campus, the food, my classes, and what I wore on the first day. Aunt El asked me why I didn't represent for the natural Chi-town girls. I laughed and reminded her of Rancho. She snickered.

"Oh...yeah, we want good lasting impressions instead of mockery, especially in the sea of potential boyfriends, LOL," she said.

I just laughed then walked into my room to get my own cell phone.

"It's been real, but this freshman has to go and get that homework done, LOL," I said.

We all laughed before I passed the phone back to my Mom. She continued to talk with my Aunts and cook dinner. I sat at the counter and checked the messages on my phone.

There were several messages from Jence and Renee. They wrote about the remainder of their afternoon, homework questions, and tomorrow's outfit selections. I told them about my fiasco in history with Mr. History. I also told them how those lemons quickly turned into lemonade—when my mystery guy tried to make me feel better. I read and replied to a few of their messages then moved on to some messages from Jaya. Once I replied to a few of Jaya's messages, I internally agreed to a few more. Next, I read some messages in a group chat from the L.O.L.s about their first days of school. They had been in school a week now and eager to hear about my first day. I immediately fessed up about wearing my hair straight—instead of naturally curly. Encountering another Rancho and Girl Scout situation in high school was just not something I was willing to sign up for. Some of them totally understood and sent pictures of their first day of school looks. They also wore well groomed, straight manes. We swapped stories about the good, bad, and disastrous styles that some people had the nerve to wear. High school is a place where you definitely don't want to have a bad day; it could haunt you forever in life. Once I told them about my History mystery, the text messages really flooded in. The messages were too much to keep up with while trying to complete my homework. I quickly let them know he was just pleasing to look at. It was only the first day of school. I exited the group—by putting the conversation on mute—as Mom checked in on me.

"Are you working on your homework or letting everyone in the world—except for *me*—know how your first day of high school was?" she asked.

"I'm working on my homework, *mom*," I said.

She looked at me with one eyebrow raised in disbelief. "Bring me that phone until your homework is done to help you focus," Mom said.

I contested but gave in. The last thing I needed to do was fall behind in the beginning. That was not an option. Besides, I was in no mood to disagree with her.

I finished my homework. Mom had just finished setting the table for our taco bar night. It was freshly made fish tacos with guacamole, salsa, and rice. As we sat down to eat, all you could hear were plates and forks clinking and scraping. Mom never said a word to me. I felt as if the air was getting a bit intense. I decided to break the silence.

"What's wrong?" I asked.

"What do you mean?" she replied. "You don't know?"

I was confused about what happened—since my nap. "I just woke up from a nap and finished my homework before dinner," I said. I reached up to touch my hair. "Aww, man...I forgot to tie down my hair. Does it look bad?" I asked. I jumped up to go check the mirror.

"It's fine. Sit down," she commanded. "Your hair can be fixed. *That* is not the issue. I asked you *hours* ago, how your first day of school went; you have not replied."

"What do you mean? When you gave me the phone to talk to Aunt Shonnie and EL, I spoke about my day," I said.

"That was not talking directly to me," Mom said. "You and I have shared all of your first days out here. This one is no different. I am still eager to hear *all* about your day."

"I understand that this is high school and not Rancho or Miles, however, a first day is a first day. I have been the one who's been there for you through all of them," she added. "At this stage, you should be able to feel like you can talk to me—*first!*"

I looked at her with my head tilted to the left. My ear touched my shoulder. "Are you serious right now?" I asked. "You sound like a Lifetime movie special."

I guess she didn't like that. She looked like she had just been cursed out! "Whoa, wait a minute. Is this about those questions in the car?" I asked.

"Yes," she said.

"My bad, I thought you were ear hustling when I was talking to Aunt El and nem," I replied.

I told Mom all about my day. Well, I left out the history mystery. She would be like a vampire on blood if I mentioned a boy. I indulged her and answered any questions she asked me. I didn't want her to be mad at me when I needed my hair fixed—for the remainder of the week. By Friday, I had seen enough to feel comfortable with releasing the beast to the masses, LOL. I mean, I felt comfortable enough to let my hair be free and not conformed to the flat-irons, bonnet, and scarf. Besides, I wanted to get some of that *Nyquil commercial* sleep. I was still adjusting to the demanding homework I was getting. Over the weekend, Mom asked me when I was anticipating for her to wash my hair—so that she could plan time to re-do it. I told her I would be going *natural* for a while. She paused.

"I'm sorry, you gone do what?" she asked.

"I am going to wear my hair natural...for a while," I replied.

"Where did this come from?" she pushed.

"Well, I figured the first week I would get used to everything—classes, campus, the lunch environment, and so on—before turning my life into an 'oooh can I touch it' event," I explained. "High school throws a lot at you. I didn't want to add self-esteem issues about me, my hair, and being Black into the mix. I just wanted to have a normal experience—no questions or defenses asked or needed."

"I get it," she said. "Well, thank the Lord for me having a break."

She turned and walked toward her room.

"...and please know you will still be required to be ready on *time*," Mom stated. "I don't want any hair left on the shower floor in your bathroom. Make sure you have enough hair care products. They should last you until you decide to switch back to straight hair, MKAY?!"

I chuckled and agreed.

Now that dinner was over, Mom was informed and content. My homework was also complete. I went into my room and focused on how the Naturally Curly Haired Black girl was about to show the campus how to properly rock *fierce* curls and clothes, LOL. There I go...being silly. I grabbed my phone and started a web of conference calls with the L.O.L.'s. We discussed what our new lives delivered and offered us as freshmen and teens. We talked for hours and swapped stories about one another's campuses, class schedules, teachers, how far we had to walk, our freshman mixers, cafeteria food, and how we made our grand entrance. I told them about the music—which played during lunch. I was the only one who experienced that privilege. In addition to our regular cafeteria food, we had food trucks come to our campus each day. Everyone else either had the standard cafeteria food—sandwiches, burgers, pizza, salad, nuggets, fruit or snack bar—or off campus lunch. Personally, off campus lunch was the best of all. At one point, we discussed how we were feeling about being in high school as Black girls—Black girls with curly hair. For those of us who were at a new school, we discussed how being alone to experience all of it made us feel.

One of my L.O.L. sisters, Natalie, told us she decided to wear her hair naturally curly once she began our Lady of the Trinity Girls School. She thought it would be no big deal because she saw several Black girls when she attended their "looksee" preview day. Our phones were dead quiet as she talked. We were quiet because Ms. Jackson provided us with an interactive demonstration on how it looks and feels when someone is sharing an experience or feelings and others are not being respectful, empowering, and considerate—should the situation call for it. I was taking notes as Natalie was sharing. I wanted to be able to respond in a positive manner to specific things that stood out. Anyway, Natalie told us that once she walked into the building to begin her day, she did not see one person with a different hairstyle—beyond the normal straight and shiny. She thought everyone was looking at her, admiring how her afro held up. She told us she later found out—from two classmates sharing over the bathroom stalls—that she was being made fun of.

There was a long pause.

"Hello, ya'll still there?" she questioned.

All you could hear were sounds of agreement. I jumped in to help Natalie.

"First of all, Nat, no one knows better than Destiny and I about being the first Black big curly haired girl on campus. I'll be more specific. I know two times over...how it feels. You all know that I have shared this with the group. You are beautiful! Your hair is Gorge, OK? And you are mad talented when it comes to your artistry skills. Day one of anything—alone—can be challenging, scary, and make you wanna clam up. I hated, *hated*, HAAAATED my hair after I wore my afro that one time because I was made fun of. Even though I was a little bit more comfortable in middle school, I still had haters and jokesters. That all made me feel *so* ugly. Had it not been for all of us coming together, I would still be a *mess*. I would have low self-esteem, no pride in a *fabulous natural black girl*. I would not have been able to be successful out here in Arizona—without my support system. I also would not be so accepting of all that comes my way—good, bad, and indifferent. Girl, we will *always* have to face some kind of problem because of small-minded people in this world. *We* just have to keep ourselves focused on obtaining our goals and dreams while *rockin that natural afro*. *Just* because I make the decision to put on the look of conformity, it does not define who *I am*. I know who Ari is. Remember who you are...everyday...all day, *Natalie*," I concluded.

"*Wow*, Ari, you snapped," said Destiny.

We all laughed and agreed with my words of encouragement.

"Ari, wrap up that call, Sugah. It's almost ten o'clock," Mom bellowed.

"Ok," I replied.

I sat and talked with the girls for a few more minutes. Natalie jumped in and thanked us for putting her back in her Black mind, LOL. We agreed that every first and third Friday of each month, we would go Natural Big and Proud. Additionally, we would post it in our snapchat group while on campus at our lunch hour. We also made a date to stop in on the middle school sisters—to see how our legacy was continuing. We expressed our gratitude (grat-it-tude) and love for one another then ended the call.

"Are you done," Mom said.

"Yes, Mom, I'm done," I replied.

"Is everything okay with Natalie?" she asked. "Is she at the 'all girls' catholic school?"

"Yeah, she's at Our Lady of the Trinity School," I replied. "She was being made fun of for wearing her natural afro to school."

"Aww, I overheard what you were saying," Mom said. "Where did that young lady who was *snapping* come from?" Mom inquired. She tried to snap and pop her neck at the same time.

"Please don't ever do those two things together in public," I teased. "I guess it came from all the experiences I had to deal with—since the moment we landed here."

"Well, I am impressed and proud of you," she said. "Now go to bed."

Chapter 19

Ari was on the phone with Destiny. They were reminiscing about that day, while she waited for Natalie to meet her in front of Miles Middle School. They were going to surprise Ms. Jackson and the current L.O.L. girls with a visit, tales of high school—now that they were juniors and driving—and leave them with words of encouragement.

"Destiny, this girl is gonna be late to her own funeral," I said. I exhaled and laughed. "How long have you been waiting?" I asked.

"Well, send her a text and see where she is," Destiny suggested.

"I did while we were talking," I said.

"Well, don't keep the girls and Ms. Jackson waiting. They will be out of school soon. The sooner you finish, the sooner you can come scoop me and we can get some shopping done," Destiny stated.

In order to drive, she had to retake her test and pass.

I hopped out the car and checked my hair, outfit, and make-up using the shadow of my car door. As soon as I stepped in the office, everyone was excited to see me. They greeted me with warm hard hugs and asked me a ton of questions about school, college, and driving. I signed in, grabbed a name tag, and headed back to Ms. Jackson's class—to surprise her and the L.O.L. girls. It looked like the lights were off in the room. I spoke to some familiar teachers roaming on-campus. I finally opened the door to Ms. Jackson's classroom.

Surprise!

It was everyone, including Natalie. I was speechless.

"Hey, what is going on here?" I asked.

"Well, we thought it would be a nice surprise to...well surprise *you*," she said. "You do so much for us and make us feel special. We wanted to do the same for you."

I looked around the room at all the Beautiful Natural Black faces, the cake, flowers, and big card envelope. I put my hand on my forehead and was truly surprised. I thanked everyone. They each rushed to hug me. We cut into that cake and had ourselves *Lots of Laughs*. Before Natalie and I left, they presented me with my flowers and a gift card to my *favorite* place, LUSH!

"Thank you so much, guys. I really appreciate it," I said. "I have to get going, but I will be looking for you all at the YBC this weekend!"

As I hugged Natalie good-bye and got back into my car, my phone rang.

"Hello," a voice said.

"Hey," I replied.

"So, how'd it go?" he said.

"We made *history*," I ended.